1st Ed

Pigeon Spring

Special Limited Edition

From Herman Groman's
Private Collection

FIRST EDITION

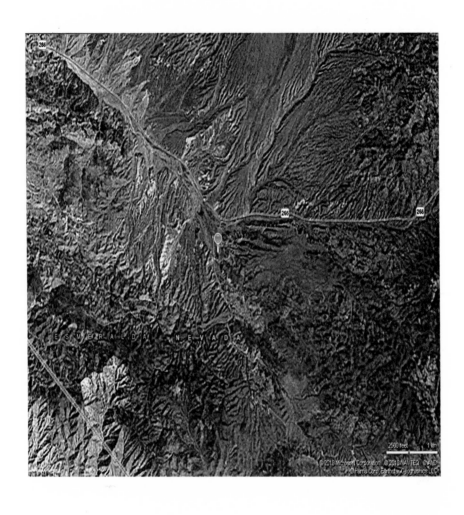

TotalRecall Publications, Inc.

United States of America
Canada
United Kingdom

Pigeon Spring

Herman Groman

ISBN: 978-1-59095-750-9

UPC: 6-43977-17504-5

This is a work of fiction. The characters, events, views, and subject matter of this book are either the author's imagination or are used fictitiously. Any similarity or resemblance to any real people, real situations or actual events is purely coincidental and not intended to portray any person, place, or event in a false, disparaging or negative light.

Printed in the United States of America with simultaneously printings in Canada, and United Kingdom.

1   2   3   4   5   6   7   8   9   10

FIRST EDITION

To Colleen

Who has always insisted that I do right even when I didn't want to: Who showed me how when I didn't want to know: Who always told me what I didn't want to hear: Who loved me best when I needed it most: And who has kept me reasonably well dressed.

Acknowledgment

There are many supports that carried this book from start to finish. My family and friends that ran from the sight of me with a new manuscript in hand. They read the updates anyway and made their helpful comments.

David M. Graham:

David your artistic and intriguing graphic design for the book cover is awesome. You are a real talent!

Jamie Carpenter aka Redpengirl

Many thanks to Jamie for your editing expertise and guidance throughout the production of the Pigeon Spring work.

John Wills Author of the Chicago Warriors Thriller Series: *Chicago Warriors Midnight Battles, Gripped by Fear and Targeted.*

A special thanks to John for introducing me to our publisher Bruce Moran with his team of experts. It couldn't have happened without you brother.

About the Book

Pigeon Spring is an exciting modern day western mystery with a mystical twist, where the reader follows retired FBI Agent and now casino security director Matt Steel, from the glamour and scams at a Las Vegas casino to the beauty and grit of Nevada's rugged gold country and his dealings with the plentiful scoundrels found where-ever money is to be made.

Table of Contents

Acknowledgment iv
  About the Book v
  Preface vii
CHAPTER 1: THE CONNECTION 1
CHAPTER 2: THE RANCH 5
CHAPTER 3: THE NEIGHBORS 12
CHAPTER 4: THE SCULPTOR 34
CHAPTER 5: THE TRAIL RIDE 43
CHAPTER 6: THE NEW PARTNERS 49
CHAPTER 7: SPRINGTIME 56
CHAPTER 8: THE INVESTORS 70
CHAPTER 9: BACK TO WORK 74
CHAPTER 10: THE HOLIDAY WEEKEND 83
CHAPTER 11: THE RECORDS 89
CHAPTER 12: THE FAVOR 91
CHAPTER 13: THE SURVEILLANCE 95
CHAPTER 14: THE INVESTIGATION 105
CHAPTER 15: THE CONFRONTATION 110
CHAPTER 16: THE RECORDS 119
CHAPTER 17: TURN IN THE ROAD 125
CHAPTER 18: THE NEWCOMERS 129
CHAPTER 19: THE SALES PITCH 139
CHAPTER 20: A MOUNTAIN OUT OF A MOLEHILL 149
CHAPTER 21: A TANGLED WEB 154
CHAPTER 22: ALL THAT GLITTERS 160
CHAPTER 23: THE ROUNDUP 167
CHAPTER 24: THE AFTERMATH 174
CHAPTER 25: BACK TO NORMAL — *SORT OF* 179
CHAPTER 26: OBSTACLES 190
CHAPTER 27: THE STRUGGLE 193
CHAPTER 28: GATHERING WOOD 203
CHAPTER 29: IMPROBABLE ALLIES 209
CHAPTER 30: THE MEETING 214
CHAPTER 31: REAWAKENING 222
CHAPTER 32: RESOLUTION 225
CHAPTER 33: SAYING GOODBYE 228
EPILOGUE 232
  About the Author 234

Preface

You have noticed that everything an Indian does is in a circle, and that is because the power of the world always works in circles, and everything tries to be round ... The sky is round, and I have heard that the earth is round like a ball, and so are all the stars. The wind, in its greatest power, whirls. Birds make their nest in circles, for theirs is the same religion as ours ... Even the seasons form a great circle in their changing, and always come back again to where they were. The life of a man is a circle from childhood to childhood, and so it is in everything where power moves.

Black Elk, Oglala   Sioux Holy Man

The FBI had become a part of him. It wasn't all of him. He was a lot of other things too. He was a husband, a father, a grandfather, a son, a brother, and a veteran. He was a friend to some and to a few, a hated bastard, but just a few. Now he was a director of security for a Las Vegas casino and hotel. Life was a series of building blocks: One on top of the other, each one dependent on the other. He wouldn't have the position if he hadn't been an FBI agent for twenty-five years. He wouldn't have been an agent if he hadn't gone to college after serving in Vietnam, and he couldn't have attended college if he hadn't been drafted into the army. But none of it would have happened if he had never met Alex: Especially the mystical journey called Pigeon Spring.

CHAPTER 1: THE CONNECTION

As she walked the ridge looking down at the ground, like she always did, she saw it — just laying there next to the old twisted pinion pine. It was like whoever made the thing left it there the day before. Last night's rain was over, but the wind was still blowing strong. Of course at 6500′ elevation there would be days like this. Alex had walked the same path countless times in her never-ending quest. She wondered for a moment if the object was just made or if somebody recently lost it. After all, how could she miss the gleaming find? As she bent down to get a closer view, she looked for the footprints of the poor fool who lost it. Then she remembered, they had been at the cabin for the last four days and hadn't seen anyone except the old Shoshone logger driving his beat-up F150 down the dirt road past the spring. Maybe it was his, and his footprints were washed away by last night's rain. Anyway, it was on her property, so it was now hers. The thought made her laugh. She reminded herself of Gollum from the Lord Of The Rings, "My prescioussss." This might be the best one yet. She approached the object cautiously, with a crime scene investigator's mindset. She was always amazed at the skill of the ancient sculptors, but this one was exquisite. The obsidian had a depth to it that she had never seen. *She still hadn't yet picked it up.*

Looking down from the ridge, toward the corrals, Alex could see Matt and her grandson, Thomas, nailing up some loose boards that the gelding had kicked down during last night's storm. They bought the ranch so they could have somewhere to relax on the weekends, but it seemed like there was always something to build or fix. Alex never understood, but Matt always said he found the never-ending work and projects somehow recuperative. And the place was perfect for Tommy, too. He could dig, get dirty, mess around in the pond, and do all of the boy stuff that a nine-year-old boy should do. The younger grandkids would find it to be the same as soon as they were old enough.

"Wo! OO!" "Wo! OO!" Alex cupped her hands and signaled "the boys" from on top of the ridge. The overture was a tribute to her longtime deceased special aunt, Aunt "Duck." She used it to call the cows in at their Ohio dairy farm many years in the past. It had been at least twenty years since she had died and Alex still mourned Aunt Duck. She probably would for the rest of her life.

Matt did his best "Wo! OO!" back, but he was weak in that department. Oh well, at least he gave it his best shot. Tommy just thought Papa and Nana were kind of funny in an old people sort of way, but he loved them anyway, just the way they were. Matt knew that she must have found something because she hadn't been gone that long and a "Wo! OO!" wasn't warranted at this point. Thirty-five years of marriage had taught him something about her. And now he chuckled to himself. She motioned for him to climb up on the ridge. Easy for her, she took the trail from the cabin that they had made a couple of years ago for when they got really old and wouldn't be able to climb the steep terrain. If he was going to join her, he had to take the steep route over near the cottonwood trees next to the spring.

As Alex knelt next to the object, the sun was now positioned in such a manner that she could see the center ridge running the length of it from the perfectly chiseled cutouts to just above the area where the sculptor started the elegant thinning leading toward the all-important point. This is where most failed. Her pulse quickened. *She still had not touched it.* By all accounts, the relic was a cascade: an ancient design so flawless that it remained virtually unchanged for ten thousand years.

It took about ten minutes for Matt and Tommy to climb the steep incline and get to the spot where Alex stood.

Matt loved the westward view from here. This time of year snow came early to the Sierra Nevada, but it was still Indian summer at Pigeon Spring. The snow-capped peaks in the distance stood in stark contrast to the cloudless brilliant blue Nevada sky. Thomas started to jog toward Alex; "What'd you find, Nana; another Indian rock?" He'd been on countless backcountry hikes with Alex looking for artifacts since he was five years old. Matt was more content to stay behind and tend to the ranch work, which really meant messing around, rather than tramp around the endless hills, gullies, and meadows in her never-ending obsession. *She still had not yet picked it up.* As Thomas drew near her, he started instinctively to reach toward the black masterpiece. Even at his tender age he knew it was something special. Alex reached her arm out in front, stopping him just short of the object.

By now Matt joined them and Alex pointed to it. He wondered why she had not yet picked it up. She looked at her husband and he knew immediately what she was thinking. *The connection.* She remembered when they visited the "Wall" for the first time, when she saw Matt tenderly touch the names of his fallen comrades from so many years ago. Somehow it made him connected to them once again. She thought for an instant that this was the true beauty of their long-term marriage and friendship. *The connection.* Thomas was fit to be tied, and tried his best to get between his grandmother and the object, but Alex held her ground. Matt called for his grandson to back off, and when he did, she picked it up. *The connection* had been made.

Now she was part of it. The sculptor, the warriors who used it, the flesh of the animals it had pierced. Those who had possessed it — All of them. Now she was *connected.*

The serrated edges of the spearpoint were still as sharp as any of her best Chicago cutlery. How masterful the sculptor was. What a great artisan he must have been. How was it possible that such a beautiful object could be crafted with such archaic and primitive tools? If he were born in a different time and place, would he be a Michelangelo or a Picasso? Was he a great leader of his people, or just a highly respected craftsman? What happened to him? Who was he? Did a wounded mule deer carry the spearhead in his rib cage until he outran his pursuer and then died? Where has this masterpiece been for the centuries? The questions were endless and impossible to answer. This is what fueled her impossible obsession.

CHAPTER 2: THE RANCH

The pond was dredged out last year by Raymond and was now stocked with large-mouth bass and pan fish. The state fish biologist Matt conferred with had suggested this combination. The smaller pan fish would feed the bass, and both would feast on the ever-present insects. Alex, always the animal lover, was totally against Matt stocking the pond, unless he promised not to catch and eat the fish. Catch and release was the best he could get out of her. In fact he had made a wooden sign in his work shop that was posted up at the cabin site that read, "Alexandra's Hunting Lodge — Where Animals are Never Killed and Only Rarely Eaten."

Raymond, however, was another matter. Alex and Matt had met him a few years ago when he wandered in on horseback. He was rounding up wild cattle that were the offspring from several generations ago when their place was part of the Lida Ranch cattle operation. The pond then was only a couple of feet deep, and was used to water the livestock. Over the years the debris from the cotton wood trees and sagebrush, along with the weeds and watercress, had turned it into little more than a swamp. Raymond, a rail thin cowhand/wildlife expert/tree trimmer/handyman/heavy equipment operator/folklore expert and philosopher was one of those rare breeds you almost never see anymore. When Matt and Alex were growing up in the foothills of the Appalachian Mountains in eastern Ohio, there seemed to be many such people. Matt always admired these men, both for their independence and their versatility. They made do with what they had. He missed them. Raymond lived with his wife Linda, the female version of himself, over in Gold Point about twenty miles away. Gold Point had all of seven residents, no store, no gas station, no church, but they had a saloon.

Down the stagecoach road about a half a mile from the pond was the prize, the wooden monolith that first caught Matt and Alex's eye and piqued their pursuit in acquiring the ranch. From the main road, you could see it if you knew it was there. Otherwise the structure blended in with the rising hills, sagebrush, and pinion pine. Men's fortunes, dreams, and sweat were all right there. The timbers were enormous and obviously not from around the area. They towered above the ten-foot carved stone block wall and were at least four feet in diameter. They must have been harvested from over near Mammoth Lake or Lake Tahoe well over a century ago. What a feat it would have been just to get them to this site.

The Pigeon Spring Gold Stamp Mill was located here. It operated throughout the 1890s until 1907. The accompanying settlement had a saloon, store, and a roadhouse. If he closed his eyes and imagined, Matt thought he could still hear the faint sounds of the machines, the grunting of the workmen, the clinking of whiskey bottles, and the laughter of the whores and men they entertained.

The Pigeon Spring Stamp Mill was typical of the old gold mining camps of Nevada and California that sprung up out of the dry deserts and wild mountains of the old west during the late nineteenth and early twentieth centuries. The camps and towns literally appeared overnight. The discovery of gold and silver, and in some cases, just the rumor of the precious metals created a fervor that spread like a wild fire with a back wind.

People from all walks of life flooded into these boomtowns. It was an eclectic mix of businessmen, prospectors, gamblers, hustlers, thieves, and loose women. Even a preacher or two made the trek, just in case some poor soul needed savin'. They all came with a lust this country had never before witnessed. The mining camps were harsh. The men and women were hard. These were not places for women and children or the weak and timid. Instead of wooden houses, they lived in tents and makeshift one-room stone hovels with dirt floors.

Matt was reminded of when he first saw the outskirts of Quon Loi in Tay Nin Province, Vietnam, just outside the 1st Cavalry compound back in January of 1969. The makeshift bars, hooches, and vendors ... the Saigon "tea girls" all hustling a buck. "Hey G.I., you give me ten dolla, I love you long time." It must have been much the same here back then. Under the dense sagebrush Matt saw the signs of their lives. An old rusted out baking powder can ... the broken neck of a whiskey jug ... a worn out mule shoe. Over by the mill site the place was littered with unnamed and forgotten metal thingamajigs that must have been essential to the operation of the mill.

About a hundred yards east of the mill, nestled among the sparse sage about twenty five yards on the north side of the logging road was perhaps the most intriguing and thought-provoking site of all. A headstone, stated simply: NANCY WALKER – BORN 1884 – DIED 1906. Matt had checked the Esmeralda County records in the county seat at Goldfield, some sixty-five miles to the north, a couple of years ago to no avail. Back then Dee Hunter was still alive, and Matt had even run him down to see if he could shed any light on the mystery. After all, Dee had made and placed the headstone on the grave. Back then the only thing Dee could enlighten Matt on was that he remembered seeing the original gravestone some fifty years earlier when he ran cattle for the Lida Ranch with a bunch of other cowhands.

Dee said he was about twenty-two then, the same age that Nancy was when she died, and he had always felt sorry for her, even though she had died some sixty years before, and he had never even met her. Dee wondered then, as Matt did now. "Who was she?" "How did she die?" "Was she pretty?" "Why was she here?" One night in Goldfield at the Santa Fe Saloon after three shots of Hiram Walker, Dee told Matt that he secretly fantasized about her. He sheepishly revealed that he might have loved her if he had known her back then. He stopped back at the grave about twenty years ago when a group of rich fellas from either New Jersey or New York were lookin' to bag a lion, and he was their guide. He was givin' them the grand tour when he noticed that the old grave marker was washed away by one of those one hundred year flash floods. It saddened him. He felt as if somebody had insulted her and he needed to come to her defense. So he made her a new headstone, and every now and then he stopped by just to say hello and to straighten things up. Although he tried ever since he first came across Nancy Walker, Dee was never able to get any of his questions answered. Matt suspected he wouldn't get any answered either. Matt thought it ironic. Just like Nancy Walker, these camps and towns died before they even had a chance to live. They were — and then they weren't. They were gone!

Pigeon Spring could have been different if the compelling yellow metal had not been the calling voice that made them come. There was water here. It was why the ancient Timbisha came here. It was because of the water that the pinion pines and their life-sustaining nuts were here. It was because of the water that the Nummu lived here. Water was why first Wadziwob and later Wovoka performed their sacred Ghost Dance here. Water was the reason that the mule deer, the jackrabbits, the red tailed hawks, and the feral cattle were here. It was why the cowboys came and went. It was why the U.S. Cavalry came here. It was the water. Matt and Alex were here for a different reason. *They were here because of it all.*

Ten miles in either direction, it was a very different land. To the east and south the mountains gave way to the lower elevations of the brutal Mojave Desert with its creosote and yucca. The same distance to the north put you on the road toward Silver Peak and its barren rocks. Another ten miles to the west past the Last Chance range was a steep plunge into one of the most inhospitable places on earth … Death Valley. It was no wonder that the cool elevation, trees, abundant wildlife, and *water* propelled mankind and animalkind to this place.

When Matt and Alex were looking for a weekend retreat and eventually a summer spot to live when they finally really retired, they almost passed it by. Alex said that if they were going to stay in Las Vegas, they had to get out of town during the scorching summers. It wasn't for her. It was for her horses and her dogs. Alex never really meant to have four horses and two dogs. They just sort of happened.

She never forgot her childhood roots growing up on her father's dairy farm. She remembered the animals too: Manard, Cow-Cow Boogi, and her palomino, Whiskey. They were long gone, but the memories were not.

When Matt joined the FBI over twenty-seven years ago, new Special Agents weren't sent to the countryside. New agents were going to the nation's largest cities, where the real problems were. Places like New York, Miami, Chicago, and LA. After a short stint in Pittsburgh, Matt got assigned to Detroit. At the time, the city held the dubious distinction of being the murder capital of the United States. There weren't many dairy farms there. So Alex's roots and any chance to get back to them had to take a rear seat to Matt's assignments. At least her career as a registered nurse was in demand everywhere. No matter where they were transferred, she always could find work. And with the kids, she could work different shifts to accommodate their school schedules along with Matt's.

Looking back, it seemed hectic, but at the time, they just seemed busy. Pittsburgh, Detroit, and finally Las Vegas, and all of the special assignments in between; it all seemed to fly by. The long-term and short-term undercover projects that took Matt to places like LA, Minneapolis, St. Louis, Seattle, Atlanta, Milwaukee, and Portland all seemed wound up together like the rubber bands inside a golf ball. The work that seemed so important at the time, and it was, he was sure of it, was all now behind him. He remembered when he was a new agent attending the obligatory retirement parties, and some old fart would get up and talk about how they couldn't believe where the time went. But it was true! Where did the time go? The old farts were right, and now he was one of them. An old fart. If he said it fast, it didn't sound so bad. Except for the couple of years he was assigned to work undercover in the mafia sting with "Fat Tony" when he first got sent to Las Vegas, at least he had taken good care of his body. He still did his three-mile jog every morning. Alex still looked good, too. She started working out even before Matt joined the FBI and she had kept it up. That, along with riding and shoveling the ever-present horseshit kept her looking years younger than she was. People were always amazed when they found out she had four grandchildren. Matt always jokingly said that he "over-married" and she "under-married."

Three years ago, after he retired from the Bureau, Matt took a job as Chief of Security at one of the larger hotel/casinos in Las Vegas. They always made a good living, but with his full retirement benefits, and Alex's salary, along with the salary of his new position, it was a chance to buy a few toys before they "retired-retired." One of the first things they did was buy the ranch. Now, finally, Alex could get back to where she wanted to be. Her well-deserved roots.

So here they were. Pigeon Spring, Nevada. The place was a constant reminder of how fleeting life really is. As Matt climbed the ridge again and looked out toward the mill site and then south toward the cottonwood trees, just as those countless and nameless people had done so before him, he remembered all of these things, and why they were here.

CHAPTER 3: THE NEIGHBORS

"Thomas! If you're going to go into the pond, then at least take your shoes and socks off and roll up your pants." Alex admonished him. She looked at Matt and just shook her head and gave him a slight grin, careful not to let Thomas see. He was always testing the limits. It's what boys his age were supposed to do and it seemed like he was the poster child for limit-testers.

"Okay Nana!" Thomas yelled back. Of course by then he was soaked to just below his knees. Oh well, Alex thought, it wasn't like they had any place to go, and with the low humidity, his shoes and socks would probably be dry in an hour anyway. Alex thought it was one of the great things about being a grandmother. You had a different perspective. You had the experience of raising children behind you. You knew when it was important to win the battle and when it wasn't. Because you had breathing room between visits, you had patience that you didn't have when it was a twenty-four seven responsibility. And you loved the children just as if they were yours. It was another chance.

Matt went back down to the corrals to check on Brio, the palomino gelding. He was outnumbered three to one by the mares and was always in trouble with them. It was his own fault. They gave him all the warning signs that it was time to knock off whatever irritating thing he was doing. They swished their tails and laid back their ears. The mares would sometimes even bare their teeth at him or lunge for him like they were going to take a hunk of horsehide out of him. And sometimes they did. He just didn't care. It was far more important for him to harass them in spite of the painful consequences.

He was too smart for a horse. Back in Las Vegas at their small ranchette a chain had to be kept on his corral because he had figured out how to unlatch the gate. He could do it almost as quickly as Matt could. Matt recalled a couple of years ago watching the horse take a long drink of water and when Matt walked by him five minutes later, Brio spit the water down his back and took off running. If he were a person he would have been a juvenile delinquent who would eventually end up in jail. He wouldn't be an ordinary bank robber or a car thief. He'd probably be a white collar criminal, involved in an international investment fraud or a large Ponzi scheme. Nevertheless, he was great to ride, except for the occasional gleeful buck. With Alex's help, Matt had learned to tell when he was just about to do it and was able to make a pre-emptive move that took the looming buck out of him. It was interesting though; somehow he knew if a green rider got on and didn't have the experience to deal with him. So he was a real 'gentleman' until the rider became experienced. Then the games would start. For a while, until Matt learned how to take the buck out of him, he called the horse Buckingham.

Matt was kind of proud of the horse shelter he and Alex put up a few years ago. They dug four enormous holes by hand for the supporting timbers one weekend and erected the superstructure by themselves. It almost collapsed on them at least twice until they were able to get the timbers stabilized. Once they were able to get some rock and dirt back into the holes, they had to play a game of up and down the ladder to get it level. They probably should have had Raymond or Charlie help them that weekend, but they didn't. Matt was always amazed at the amount man's work Alex could handle. She was just a little shit, too. Only 5'3" and 115 lbs. She never shied away from attempting anything physical. God knew what he was doing when he built her. Matt couldn't imagine her at 5'9" 140 lbs. She'd be dangerous!

Charlie started coming to the ranch with Matt on the weekends when Alex couldn't make it and Matt renamed him "Chuck Wagon Charlie" because of the way he could navigate the Dutch oven. They had been partners at the bureau from the first day Matt had reported to the Las Vegas office of the FBI. First on a public corruption squad, and later, on the Special Operations Group (SOG) where Charlie was the team leader and Matt was the assistant team leader. It was the covert squad that did the bureau's sneaky work. With Charlie's background of working the terrorist Macheteros group in Puerto Rico and Matt's extensive undercover background, the bad guys didn't have a chance. Since the events of 9-11, the special squad supported covert operations directed against suspected cell groups and their believers wherever they were. It was interesting work and took them to a lot of out-of-the-way places.

Matt laughed to himself when he thought about the reason Charlie decided to retire the same day as he did. Matt told the SOG team members that he was going to retire in the spring just before his birthday when he reached the mandatory age. Charlie was just a couple of months younger than Matt and he, too, would have to go shortly after him. Early one morning when the team was set up on a bad guy on the west side of Vegas, Matt launched his devious plan. They had worked together so long and knew each other's habits so well that Matt knew that if the bad guy had not yet moved by 8:30 a.m., there was about a 95% chance that Charlie would go to the nearby McDonald's to take a piss and get a cup of coffee to go.

Sure enough, at exactly 8:30a.m. Charlie announced on the Bureau radio that he was going to be 10-7 for a few minutes. What Charlie didn't know was that in anticipation of his actions, Matt sent a couple of agents with video cameras to set up on Charlie at the McDonald's. What else Charlie didn't know was that Matt had a duplicate key for Charlie's undercover Camero. As soon as Charlie went inside, Matt walked over to Charlie's Camero and stole it. He parked it behind a nearby Lowe's and waited for the panic to set in. Charlie's whole Bureau life was in the car: his FBI credentials, his MP-5 submachine gun, and a whole lot of secret documents. Even though the FBI vehicles had special alarms, they could still be broken into and stolen. Five minutes later, Charlie walked out happily carrying his steaming hot coffee. The look on his face captured on the video was priceless.

After walking around the parking lot thinking he was having a senior moment, the real panic set in. "Matt!" Charlie called on the Nextel private channel, trying not to sound like his life was about to be turned upside down because of his "negligence." (It didn't matter in the Bureau if something wasn't your fault; it was still always you fault.) "Some son of a bitch took my Bucar," Charlie yelled. Try as he could, he couldn't control his distress.

Matt responded, "Holy shit Charlie!" "All of your shit was in the car!" Matt realized that he had better end this quickly before Charlie had a coronary, or worse yet, called 911. He raced back down to the "crime scene," picked up Charlie, and took him to where the guys were gathered watching the video.

It was hilarious for everyone. Even Charlie managed to chuckle a little bit.

After the comedy show was over, they all went back to their respective surveillance locations, thankful that the real scumbag had not yet moved. Charlie took up a spot in an apartment complex and was prepared to take him if the "eye" (the fixed surveillance agent) called out that he was moving northbound. By now the Vegas rush hour traffic was at its peak. Matt had been on high speed chases and fast-moving surveillances in unfamiliar terrain all over the globe with Charlie; Matt thought Charlie was one of the best drivers he had ever seen. This day he wasn't, probably because he was still geeked up from the scam Matt had just pulled on him.

Sure enough, the bad guy came out, got in his vehicle and the eye called it out as north bound. Charlie responded, "I'll get him," and started to accelerate from his spot in the apartment complex, plowing into the front end of a divorce attorney's Volvo, which peeled off like it was part of a tangerine. Surprisingly, nobody was hurt. Not Charlie, or the divorce attorney, who was dressed in a bathrobe and flip-flops, or his female "client," whom he was taking home from a night of "counseling." The Volvo was practically totaled. The Las Vegas motorcycle cops who responded for the report were the best. "Oh, so we have the FBI here." "And you, sir, the one with the robe, what do you do?" "Oh, I see." "You're an attorney." "Are you practicing to be a judge? Is that why you have the robe on?"Needless to say, the surveillance was over for the day.

The next day Matt went the main office to turn in his retirement papers. In the parking lot of the FBI office he saw Charlie in his Camero pull in right behind him. Matt asked, "What are you doing here?"

Charlie responded, " After what you guys did to me yesterday, the day you retire is the day I'm going. I'm done." And so Charlie retired the same day as Matt did. In fact, they had a joint retirement party.

As Matt looked at Brio the gelding, he understood Brio a little better.

"Tommy and I are going down to check on old Red," Matt yelled out to Alex. Alex was sitting at the picnic table in the shade under the cottonwood tree by the pond examining her new treasure piece with her magnifying glass. She only used the magnifying glass when her find was something spectacular like the stone pipe she found about a year ago up by Crow Chase. She named the steep foothill to Mt. Magruder about a year ago, after she had been chased by a couple of crows that were probably nesting when she came across them on one of her excursions. They squawked and dove toward her head and didn't let up until they drove her down off their homestead.

Alex yelled back, "Make sure you guys get back around feeding time, because Raymond and his wife, Linda, said they might stop by on their way back from Fish Lake Valley." If they did, Alex was going to ask them to stay for ribs and beans. Raymond was doing some dozer work, clearing some pads that a Canadian gold mining company was using to test for deep deposits. Fish Lake Valley was about thirty miles northwest of Pigeon Spring. The ranch was about halfway between Fish Lake Valley and Gold Point where Raymond and Linda lived and they had to pass Pigeon Spring on their way home. Linda often went out with him to give him a hand when he needed it. But mostly she went to keep him company and to go for help if Raymond got upside down. The areas that he worked in were some of the most remote sites in the lower forty-eight and help could be several hours away if it was needed. They still had not found the famed pilot James Foster who had disappeared in the area a few years ago in a small private plane, despite the intense efforts of the National Guard and all of their state-of-the-art equipment.

Old Red, a hermit-like prospector, was Matt and Alex's only neighbor, if someone who lived three miles away could be called a neighbor. Red lived by himself in a small camper trailer just off the dirt road to the abandoned mining camp of Sylvania west of Pigeon Spring. Red was probably in his mid-seventies and except for being hard of hearing, he seemed to be in good health. He was tall, too, probably 6'5," and still had good posture. It was easy to figure out why they called him "Red." He still had a healthy mane of reddish hair, although it was smattered with encroaching gray. Matt had promised Red's son, Little Red, who lived over in Fresno that he would look in on his father from time to time. Little Red tried to make the drive from Fresno every other weekend to bring his father supplies and help him with his prospecting, but he wasn't always able to make it.

Red had designed and built the ultimate sluice box, though calling it a sluice box was a vast understatement. It started with a large hopper that could hold at least two yards of excavated dirt, and was strategically located on a hillside that could be accessed by his old dump truck. The dirt and rocks in the gravity-fed hopper was assisted in its dissent by a vibrating mechanism that kept all the dirt flowing toward the conveyor belt. The conveyor belt separated the larger pebbles from the real pay dirt and took it toward a water rinse and another vibrating device that further separated the particles. At the same time the other debris was distributed to a discard pile by another conveyor belt. There were a lot of other bells and whistles that performed some vital functions Matt couldn't quite figure out. It even had a metal scaffolding and steps that Red scurried about to make sure the contraption was running at top efficiency. It was pretty impressive. All of this was powered by a specially adapted diesel generator and several electric motors. Red also pumped water to the sluice box from a well he had drilled about a half a mile away. A solar pump powered the well with several deep cycle twelve-volt batteries for back up. Red said that when he chose the site to drill for water, he read the hills and gullies for the best spot. He must have done just that, because he hit water at just twenty-seven feet. Impressive, considering this area was still part of a vast desert, even though it was much higher in elevation. He went to a hundred feet just to make sure it wouldn't run dry. Red, like Raymond, was another one of those independent and versatile men that Matt admired and missed.

Thomas liked to go anywhere in Papa Matt's F-350 four-wheel drive diesel because he was allowed to sit on Matt's lap and steer. There was one spot on the way over to Red's place that they had to use the four-wheel drive, and except for that spot, Thomas was allowed take the wheel. In fact, Thomas was getting pretty good at it.

As they approached Red's operation, a normal hearing person would have heard the big diesel truck approaching, even over the commotion generated by the sluice box. Matt guessed that besides old age, Red's exposure to the high decibel noise was a contributing factor to his hearing loss. Oh well, Matt thought. Red rarely had anybody to talk to anyway. Matt didn't like to surprise him though, and he hoped Red would see the dust plume of his truck on the way in. They approached the open gate to his property and Red saw them from where he stood on the scaffolding of the sluice box, giving them a two-fingered salute from the brim of his stained green and yellow John Deere ball cap. His eyesight was still pretty good.

"How's it going, Red?" Matt yelled. He was difficult to communicate with even without the sluice box gyrating. It always made Thomas uncomfortable when he and Papa went to visit Red, because he wasn't used to the yelling part. Somehow he equated it to somebody being in trouble. Nevertheless, he was respectful of the communication process with Red and even tried to answer some of Red's questions about how he was doing. Usually Matt had to interpret by yelling his grandson's responses back to Red, but once they all got used to it, it all seemed sort of natural. "Did you have any luck today?" Matt inquired.

Red couldn't wait to respond and scurried down from his perch on the scaffolding, all the while motioning for Matt and Thomas to follow him down to a makeshift outside workbench located near the steps next to the water intake pipe. "I'm glad you stopped by Matt; I been waitin' nine days to show Lil' Red or somebody else I can trust. Looky here." With that, Red eagerly opened an old olive drab-colored U.S. Army .30 caliber ammo can that sat on the workbench. From it he retrieved a small oil-stained rag and slowly and gently peeled back the layers of cloth as if whatever was inside the rag was as fragile as the wings of a butterfly. Matt viewed old Red's gnarled and calloused hands, respectful of the hard work and years they had seen. "Matt, I couldn't believe it. Especially just layin' in there with the placer dirt." With that, Red peeled back the rag and revealed a gold nugget half the size of a grown man's toe. Matt and Tommy both craned their necks, and for a second they jostled for best position to see it. "Ain't it pretty Matt? I never seen one like this in all these years of pokin' holes all over God's creation. And it was just layin' there in some placer dirt! Just layin' there! I didn't even have to find it sluicin'."

Matt had heard that on a good day, Red was taking out about an ounce-and-a-half of placer. At six hundred to seven hundred dollars or more an ounce, maybe he should start poking holes in the ground.

"Damn Red! That's beautiful!" Matt marveled.

Thomas pleaded, "Can I touch it please?"

"Touch it? Course you can, little fella'. Pick it up in your hand, Thomas." Red belted out.

With that, Thomas started to grab it with his nine-year old thumb and index finger and fumbled with the unexpected weight. He had to re-grip it with the remaining four fingers in order to retrieve it from the can. "Wow! I can't believe how heavy it is, Papa. Feel it." Thomas handed it to his grandfather.

Even though Matt was ready to receive the nugget's weight, he was surprised at its unexpected density. "You're right, Tommy! It's really heavy for its size. It feels like a small brick." Matt held it up in the light for a better view and examined every bump and indentation. For a moment, Matt's law enforcement imprint training started to kick in and he found himself concerned about flaunting the precious metal object around for anybody to see, forgetting that there wasn't anybody around this isolated spot for miles. "What do think it's worth, Red? It's got to be at least a half-pound."

"Yep. You're pretty close, Matt. I weighed it just the other night with my good scale. It's 9.1 ounces."

"Now that's a payday, Red. I guess you got a new infection of gold fever in you now, don't you?"

"You're darn right, Matt. After I first found it, I stayed there, diggin' in the same spot way past dark. In fact, I turned my jeep headlights on the spot and kept diggin' until past midnight. I thought about stayin' all night, but I got too hungry and came on back to camp."

Now Matt had a new worry for Red. He was always concerned that some predator scumbags might find their way into Red's operation and rob him, but now, if the word got out about his new find, no doubt it would attract trouble. Matt would have to discuss Red's need to be careful and give him some basic security advice on how he should handle this find around others he might think trustworthy.

"You know, Red, you should invest in some digging equipment if you're going to continue to do what you do. None of us are getting any younger. Just think of how you could increase production if you had at least a back hoe with a front loader or a trenching machine."

"I know you're right, Matt, but I been doin' it this way so long, well, I guess I'm just used to breakin' my back. It's probably what's kept me pluggin' along. You know they say hard work is supposta' be good for you. 'Sides, that kind of equipment costs a lot of money. I don't have that kind of cash. Even if this here new spot produces, it's still a lot of money for me. But you're right, I ain't getting' any younger."

Changing the subject, Matt said ,"Listen Red, I know you don't see many folks, but why don't you come over to the ranch tonight? Alex is doing some ribs and beans and we have way too much. In fact, I think Raymond and Linda are going to be stopping by on their way back from Fish Lake Valley and they'll probably be eating with us. It'll be like a Fourth of July picnic without the fourth or the July or the fireworks. Anyway, you need to see people every now and then, even if you have to make yourself do it."

In spite of the fact that he was well adjusted to the loneliness of his life, he knew full well Matt was right. "Well, I don't know, Matt. My clothes aren't in that great of shape. Even the good ones ain't lookin' so good. But I wouldn't mind seein' Ray and his wife again. I think it's been about four months since I last saw ' em. He was clearing some pads for that Canadian outfit he works for up past Sylvania."

"Red, you see what I've got on, including the horseshit on my boots? This is what I'll be wearing until I crawl into bed tonight."

"And look at me, Red. Nana's kind of mad at me for getting all muddy in the pond and I'm not changing clothes. Right Papa?" Hoping his grandfather would agree with his very convincing logic.

"That's right, Thomas. What d'ya say, Red?"

"Well, I could use a nice meal of ribs and beans. What time does the little woman want me over there?"

"We'll eat about six, but you can come on over any time."

"Okay. I'll be over then." Red finalized it. And with that, Matt and Thomas both climbed up into the driver's side of the F-350 with Thomas assuming his rightful place on Matt's lap and they were off.

On the way back to the ranch, as Tommy concentrated on his driving skills by biting down on his lower lip, thereby increasing his ability to keep the big truck aligned with the road, Matt began to formulate his proposal. If everyone agreed, it would be the perfect solution for several issues.

They slowly navigated through the rough spot where the four-wheel drive was needed and approached the top of the next foothill; Matt could see the entrance to the ranch about a mile off to the east. It looked like there were two vehicles parked on the ranch road next to the corrals. One looked like Ray's old blue and white Chevy pick-up and Matt couldn't quite make out the other one. From the distant profile nomenclature, it looked like a dark-colored SUV of some sort. As they got about a half-mile closer, Matt confirmed that it was a dark blue Dodge Durango, and he could see several figures milling around the vehicle like they were checking it out. Matt could tell from the body language of all those present that there wasn't any problem and he felt immediate relief.

As he drew closer, he could make out the distinct body features of Alex, Raymond, Linda, and Charlie. His ingrained SOG surveillance days would never leave him. What was Charlie doing here? Maybe he just wanted to get away from Vegas for a day or two. Then it became clear. The new Dodge Durango was his new car, and he probably wanted to drive it somewhere. They had a lot of food, but he wasn't sure they had enough for everyone. What the hell, they would make do. As they drove past the old mill site and came within honking distance, Thomas laid on the irresistible horn. "Hey Papa. That looks like Charlie. He must have gotten a new car."

"What's up? Gloria couldn't take your obsessive compulsive disorder anymore and threw you out for a couple of days?" Happy to see his old partner.

"Yeah, she said, why don't I go up to the ranch and bother you," Charlie jabbed back. "But don't worry; I'll pay for my stay." With that, he walked around to the hatchback of the new Dodge and motioned toward the ice chest located inside. "Thought I might do a pot of my hobo stew in the Dutch oven. And if you're real nice, you might get a bite or two. Of course everybody else can eat their fill."

"Perfect, because I invited old Red over for dinner, and when I saw you, I started thinking we might be eating hay with the horses." Matt sparred. "I see you bit the bullet and got a new ride."

"Yeah. I drove the old Ford Explorer till the wheels fell off. It had about a hundred and seventy thousand miles on it. I hated to go new, but with the financing and warranty, it's tough to say no." Thomas sat on Papa's lap lusting to take the wheel of the new Dodge, but held his request in check.

"Did you bring the margarita ball?" Matt realized it was a dumb question as soon as he asked. Charlie never went on a trip without his infamous "margarita ball." It was a two-and-a-half gallon clear plastic ball shaped device with a white spring-activated pump on the top. In it was Charlie's highly-guarded secret margarita recipe, which was largely lopsided with a more than generous dose of Jose Quervo Gold. The "ball" accompanied the SOG team wherever they went, and was the centerpiece of countless debriefings in too many hotel rooms to count. In fact the "ball" probably had accumulated enough frequent flyer miles to go anywhere on the globe several times over. Charlie said the ball had mystical qualities. "Well what are we waiting for?" Matt said, and he went for some cups and ice.

Right at six o'clock sharp, and not a minute early, old Red rumbled in driving his open-top 1948 Jeep Willey's. He looked like that Pat Grady character from the old Roy Rogers movies driving old Nellie Bell. For a hermit, he didn't quite fit the profile.

By then, everybody, except Raymond and Thomas, of course, had several pumps from the ball and probably over-greeted old Red. Raymond preferred to stick with his

Budweiser and wasn't flexible with his choice of adult beverages. Matt made sure that he always had some Bud around just for these types of occasions.

Alex had the ribs already rubbed with her hickory-based salt, garlic, and cracked pepper dry rub, and was waiting on the nod from Charlie for when to put them on the Weber. Charlie had the Dutch oven hooked on the chain on the cast iron tripod hanging over the hot embers of a pinion pine fire in the outside fire pit, and the sumptuous stew was just starting to steam. Coordination was now the key ingredient in bringing the orchestration to full symphony status. It was starting to look and smell like a good time.

Red brought along some his own homemade peach brandy and Matt only hoped he had brought enough. None of them were big drinkers, but Matt had tasted Red's special brew and knew it would be irresistible to the others once they tried it. As they drank, talked, and waited, Matt asked Alex to show everyone her latest treasure. Alex was a modest person by nature. That, coupled with her sometimes-brutal honesty, were two of the attributes that first attracted him to her and continued to do so even after all the years. Surprisingly, however, and completely out of character, she jumped at the suggestion and eagerly went to retrieve her masterpiece, while unabashedly bragging about the quality of her recent find. While she was gone, Matt took the opportunity to subtlety plant the seed of his idea.

As she approached the front porch of the cabin, her pace quickened. It was like the ancient cascade and she had a magnetic pull on each other. It was something more than its sheer elegance and perfection. "My presciousss." God! She hoped she wasn't turning into Gollum! What a repulsive creature with his swampy habits. She pictured herself as Gollum slithering around the pond among the cattails holding her artifact in her skinny swamp creature fingers. She laughed at the thought. My presciousss.

By the time she got back to where the boys and Linda were all huddled around Chuck-Wagon Charlie's Dutch oven fire sipping their drinks and intently talking, Charlie made eye contact with her and signaled that the time was right to start the ribs. Red was saying, " We'll I'll tell you, Ray, I know there's a lot more out there just like this one." Matt would be concerned if Red was discussing his recent find outside this safe circle, and if it all worked as he hoped, his concerns would be moot anyway. Matt decided to let the conversation develop naturally between Raymond and Red and if it needed a gentle nudge in the direction of his hoped-for-plan, then he would pick the opportune time, and ever so discreetly, and almost subliminally, insert the stem cell of the idea into their conversation. He had honed this survival skill as an undercover agent dealing with some of the best con men and vicious wise guys the drug cartels and mob had to offer. The key ingredient was less is better. Let them think it was their idea. Manipulate the circumstances in such a way that the only logical thing for them to do was what you wanted them to do. It had to be subtle. When they took the bait, give them a mouthful and then set the hook. Matt realized that this was excessive and a bizarre way to equate this situation to his dealings with the sociopaths he encountered in his former life. He didn't like this about himself. Now that he was no longer doing this for a living, he would have to work on being less manipulative.

"Alex, you're not the only one to find something special. Look what Red has." With that Red proudly presented the beautiful gold nugget to her. It looked even more seductive in the firelight.

Alex had the same reaction as everyone else. "Wow Red! That's a nice chunk of gold!"

"You're right. Now, I only have to find a whole lot more just like it." The old man practically yelled, and then laughed as if he hadn't done so in a long time. "Hey, show us that arrowhead you found. Matt says it's a beauty!" With that, Alex eagerly presented her find for all to individually examine.

When the spearpoint made its way around to Raymond, he handled it almost reverently. He had done his own share of Native American artifact hunting and had an extensive collection of his own. Besides Alex, he had the greatest appreciation for what he now held in his hand. "It looks like an obsidian spearpoint. Probably a cascade," he said matter-of-factly. Raymond always surprised Matt with the scope of his knowledge. He didn't present himself that way. He was folksy by nature, and he never went to college. Yet, he sometimes read Shakespeare or Hemingway — after he changed the rear differential in his truck or milked his goat. But he wasn't a fake intellectual or like those who pretended to be folksy and threw in just a little bit of intellectual talk just to let you know they were smart. He was genuine.

"It's the best I've ever seen, Alex. Where'd you find it?" Alex's first instinct was to be protective of the information, but almost immediately realized who was asking and put that feeling on hold. After all, if Red wasn't fearful about his disclosure, then why should she be? Why was this her first thought of the legitimate question? She needed another margarita. "I found it right up behind the cabin just off the path on the ridge. It's a funny thing, though; I walk that ridge every day and sometimes more than once. And you know how I keep my eyes on the ground when I'm walking around," reminding her that Matt always said if she were an Indian, her name would have been 'Woman Looks Down.' "I don't know how I could have missed it all this time."

"It rained pretty hard last night. After a good storm is when I had some of my best finds," retorted Raymond.

"That's right, Ray; remember that bird point we found out near Cucamonga Spring three years ago after that big storm? It was just layin' outside the opening of our tent. We'd been in and out of that tent probably forty-six times in three days of camping and never saw it until that morning after the storm. I think a hard rain makes 'em kind of sprout up and grow out of the ground sometimes." Linda gave a little chuckle at her own joke.

After the spearpoint was passed completely around the group, which included an examination by Thomas as well, Ray commented on how he had never seen one so well preserved and sharp on the edges. "It's almost as sharp as my Barlow, and I use a wet stone on it at least once a week. It's a real beauty, Alex."

"Yep, I think I just might just keep it." And with that, she carefully wrapped it in a bundle of toilet tissue she had brought down with her from the cabin, and ever so carefully placed it in the right front pocket of her Wranglers for safekeeping. She would have to make it the centerpiece of a display and put it in a place of prominence. Maybe she would hang the display in the center of the fireplace just above the mantle on the stone chimney. That would be the perfect spot. One thing was for sure though; it couldn't ever leave Pigeon Spring! This is where it belonged.

Matt continued to monitor the ongoing conversation between Red and Raymond, listening to its direction and content. "So far, so good," he thought. Matt could tell that the line he had been waiting for was just about ready to be uttered by one of the two, or possibly both. It was just around the corner. If it weren't, he'd be surprised. This was one of his specialties.

He couldn't help recall the time when he received a desperate call from a very frustrated Jerry McCorkle. Jerry was the case agent in charge of a major organized crime investigation and Matt and the SOG team had been helping him for several months in documenting the activities of Dominic Milana. Milana was the Underboss of the Milana crime family based in southern California. After the earthquake in 1993, he and a couple of his crew members moved from L.A. to Las Vegas, and were under constant surveillance by the Bureau. Jerry had put together a complex case against him and several high-ranking members of his outfit. The Bureau was poised to execute multiple search warrants at several key locations in Las Vegas, Los Angeles, and New York on the case, and it all hinged on when Milana was scheduled to go to a VA clinic for a follow-up visit on his previous cataract surgery. Despite the fact that the Bureau had been electronically monitoring all of his conversations, they were not able to figure it out. Other factors in Los Angeles, as well as New York, dictated that they needed to move quickly when he went to the VA, and all of the warrants needed to be executed simultaneously. Several hundred FBI Agents would be involved in the operation. It was a coordination nightmare and time was getting short.

Every day at the same time, Milana went to the same Las Vegas casino race and sports book to bet the ponies, and in fact that's exactly where he was currently located as Jerry and Matt were talking with the SOG team watching him.

"Matt, this is driving me crazy. I've got all these other offices calling me every five minutes for an update, let alone headquarters in D.C. Can you think of any way we can get the information we need to get them off my back? I need to get this thing coordinated!"

"I'll call you back. I've got an idea." Matt finished the call.

After watching Milana get up from his seat in the race and sports book and place his bets with the clerk at the counter several times, Matt made the decision to take action and notified the team of his plan.

Holding a betting slip in his hand and assuming his best old-man look, Matt put on his reading glasses and got in line behind Milana at the counter. Right after Milana placed his bet, Matt said, " Excuse me. Can you help me with this? I'm having a problem reading this bet slip. I've got cataracts and I think they're getting worse." *Cataracts* must have been the magic word, because Milana sympathetically turned to Matt and said, "Sure," and read off the section of Matt's bet slip in question.

Milana followed up with, "Yeah, I know what you mean, those cataracts are a real fuckin' pain in the ass. I just had mine done not too long ago."

Matt followed with, "I know I need to get mine done, but I don't have the money for it right now."

The ever-helpful Milana then asked, "Hey! Are you a veteran? If you are, you can have it done for free. It's the only good thing those motherfuckers in the government have ever done for me. If fact, I have to go back for a check-up on Thursday morning."

By the time Matt discussed his service in Vietnam with

Milana, they were practically best buddies. Matt asked him, "What time do they open?"

"The pricks don't open for the first appointment until eight in the morning, so I got the first one." That having been said, Matt thanked Milana for the "information," and they parted company.

"Jerry, he's going to the VA this Thursday. He's got an eight a.m. appointment to get his eyes checked."

"Matt, I don't know how you got the information, and maybe I don't want to know, but I owe you big time."

The conversation needed a nudge. "Hey Ray. I hear you might have some down time for a couple of months. The word in Goldfield is that Canadian outfit might be having some financial problems, and they might have to put things on hold for a while."

"That's what the Chief Engineer told me a couple of days ago. But he said it was just a temporary situation. Said it had something to do with some investors or something. Whatever it is, I'll find something to do. Maybe I'll get some work over at that White Water Ranch development."

That having been said, Red slid his John Deere cap off his head and after scratching it several times, and then rubbing the area that he just scratched, said, "Ray, you know I been thinking, for a lot of reasons, maybe I could use a partner. I mean you got the equipment, and I got the nose for prospectin', plus you ain't gonna be doin' nothin' for a while, so I just thought we might join up with each other. What do you think?"

Ray turned toward Linda, and after an almost imperceptible reciprocating nod from her, held up his Budweiser, set it back down without taking a drink, and said: "Red, I think I'll try some of that peach brandy." Red administered all of the adults a generous pour of the homemade potion, and Raymond announced in loud voice, "I'd like to propose a toast to the new partners in the newly formed R & R Mining Company." And with that, they all clinked their drink cups together, including Tommy's box of grape juice with a straw, and the 50% partnership was born.

"They weren't the bad guys, but the technique still worked." Matt was satisfied.

"I've got a question," Thomas yelled out so Red could hear. "Does the first R stand for Red or Raymond?"

The ever-so-quick thinking Raymond drawled, "Well, I guess it depends on who's talkin' at the time!"

They all belly-laughed at Ray's joke, and Chuck-Wagon Charlie yelled out, "Let's eat!"

CHAPTER 4: THE SCULPTOR

The meat practically fell off the rib bones and it was a good thing, too, because Alex wasn't sure about how many original teeth old Red had in his head. He was missing a few, but it didn't seem to bother him. He didn't have any apparent problem with the carrots or potatoes in Charlie's hobo stew, but they were soft, too.

It didn't quite make sense. Red was such a nice man. He seemed to relate well with people and he had a good sense of humor. Alex wondered why he chose to live such a lonely life. It was probably a good thing that he was going to partner up with Raymond for several different reasons. And with Linda around most of the time, it would be a more normal existence. It would be good for Matt and her, too. They wouldn't have to worry about him so much. Neither would little Red. She would be concerned about the partnership otherwise, but they were all good and honorable people. It should work out just fine. But it sounded suspicious. It all fit too well. She suspected this had Matt's fingerprints all over it. He was always trying to set things up. He did it when the kids were growing up and there was the possibility of family problems. Always setting up situations that would make things better. She would have to ask him if he set this up. But what was the point? He would just deny it anyway, she thought, and then smiled. At least he always had good intentions, but she really wished he would just let things alone and not meddle.

Thomas sat huddled in his grandmother's arms mesmerized

by the fading embers and hypnotized by the struggling flames looking for more fuel so they could keep doing their job. With a full belly and the security and comfort of the surroundings, he couldn't help but succumb, and nodded off. Matt made eye contact with Alex and motioned that he would carry him up to the cabin. He was getting too big for her and even Matt would find it difficult to carry him up to the cabin site. She wondered how big he would eventually be when he was all grown up. She hoped she would be around to find out.

"Well I guess this party is just about over," Ray quietly announced, not wanting to wake Thomas.

Matt didn't think Red was capable of whispering, but he did and added, "You know Matt, when you told me today that I needed some equipment, I knew you was right, but I didn't think about Ray until you mentioned that thing about that Canadian outfit goin' bust." Matt could feel Alex's eyes on him.

Old Red couldn't whisper after all.

"You guys all go ahead. I'll clean this stuff up," Charlie announced. And with that, the Fourth of July party without the fourth or the July or the fireworks was over.

Charlie preferred to stay in the old camper trailer that he and Matt pulled up from Las Vegas a few years ago. They used the camper to stay in while the cabin was being built and Matt kept it for family reunions or when they had a large group of friends at the ranch for a weekend trail ride. There were two bedrooms and a loft in the cabin, so they had plenty of room for Charlie, but even though he was gregarious by nature, Matt suspected that he enjoyed just being alone occasionally, so he didn't push the idea on him. If he wanted to stay in the cabin, Charlie knew he was more than welcome to do so.

After getting Tommy into bed, Matt joined Alex on the overstuffed sofa facing the fireplace. She had just finished banking the fire for the night and was looking at her new treasure with her magnifying glass and reading glasses. Matt plopped his socked feet on the oak-paneled door that he had converted into a coffee table. They had decided even before they had the ranch that if they ever built a cabin, they would furnish it with used furniture and garage sale finds. They didn't want to have to worry about the grandkids marking something up, or a guest spilling some red wine on something. They wanted a place where they could relax. The coffee table looked rustic enough and it blended in perfectly with the rest of the furnishings. Everything looked like it belonged there.

Alex was good at this. She got up and went to the old pie safe she found left out for trash when they still lived in Michigan. It served as her library for reference books. She returned to the sofa with a large book entitled, Native American Artifacts Of The Western United States, and started her finger down the index section. When she got to the section of "Projectile Points," she opened the book to the appropriate page and found what she was looking for ... Cascade SpearPoint.

The point first appeared in the northwestern United States, west of the Cascade Mountains just after the Clovis period around 10,000 years ago. The first inhabitants of North America probably arrived in the Pacific Northwest around 2000 years earlier via a frozen ice bridge from Siberia and migrated into the Alaskan Peninsula, and eventually made their way south into North America. While the "Cascade" first made its début around that period, because of its "time tested" design, it remained a preferred spear point for several thousand years. Until around AD 500, the main weapon in North America was the Atl-atl. It was a hand-held wooden lance-thrower, and was an extension of the human arm. It provided leverage in flinging the spear further and harder. It wasn't always easy to tell the difference between a spearhead and an arrowhead. Usually it was the size of the point that made the difference. Spearheads averaged around 2 inches and about ½ inch between the basal notches. Arrowheads were closer to 1 inch or more in length and tended to be proportionately thinner than the typical spear point. The "masterpiece" was somewhere in between these dimensions.

The "Cascade" also had an intriguing and mysterious history to it. The stone point was found embedded in the pelvis of the 9000 year old "Kennewick Man," and new bone growth around it suggested that he lived for several months or years after it wounded him. In 1996, the skeletal remains of the ancient human found on the Columbia River near Kennewick, Washington, sparked a dispute between anthropologist, scientists, and local Native tribes. The Asatru Folk Assembly, a Nordic based group, also put in a claim after it was learned that the skull and leg bones resembled those of Europeans. Research into the Kennewick Man also brought to light an ancient Nevada Paiute legend about the Paiutes taking the land from the "Si-Te-Cah Tule Eaters," whom they called the "redheaded giants." One thing was for sure, the Kennewick Man" did not have the typical bone structure of the Native American face. His was smaller and set forward with an angled and jutting jawbone. This was just the kind of impossible dilemma her obsession thrived on. She would never be able to resolve it, and she loved it!

"You go ahead to bed; I'm going to do some reading. I won't be up long."

"All right. See you in the morning," Matt gave her a light

kiss on the top of her head and headed to bed for the night. Alex retrieved the "horse-themed" quilt her mother had made for her last Christmas, just for nights like this, and curled up with the book and began to intently read.

The mute relic talked for the first time in a long time.

"The chipping sound was too loud. It would frighten our four-legged brother, and make it harder for his spirit to enter our people. "Great Spirit" gave them more legs than "Our People" so they could run faster, but he gave us more wisdom. "Great Spirit" wanted us to use our wisdom. This is why he gave it to us. He also put the shiny smooth black rock here for us and guided us to this spot at this time." The sculptor decided to continue. "The others would go on without him and he would meet them where the water was. If the "Great Spirit" wanted it so, they would find their four legged brother and "Our People" would eat."

The sculptor continued with his craft.

The small collection of obsidian volcanic glass was deposited here 5.3 million years ago during the latter part of the Miocene period, when the last violent cataclysmic event took place and finally formed what is now known as Death Valley. Volcanism throughout the region provided thick ash deposits and the basin and range topography began to develop. 1.6 million year ago during the Pliocene period the alluvial fans spread into the valley and the Sierra Nevada Mountains began to rise. Mankind would not place his footprint here for many eons later, when the Nevares Spring Culture ventured into the valley replaced later by a new group of people 6000 years ago that came to be known as the Desert Shoshone. They were distinguished for their production of superior arrowheads and pottery making skills. They moved about the Death Valley region and nearby mountains hunting sheep, deer, and rabbits. During other seasons, they would harvest pinion pine nuts and mesquite beans, which sustained them when they had no meat. The mountainous area surrounding Pigeon Spring was one of their richest hunting areas and because of the plentiful and clear water from the spring, and the cooler climate; it became one of their favorite summer campsites for hundreds of years. Others called them Timbisha, but they called themselves "Our People."

Before he continued, the sculptor looked west toward the White Mountains many days travel from the flat rock where he now sat on a great and high cliff. From this place, he could see how "Great Spirit" made the light shine on a nearer mountain as it slid toward his winter home in the valley. "Great Spirit" made his promise to Our People here. He could see the promise of the deer in the shadow cast on the rocks on the lower side of the smaller mountain before it disappeared into the next valley. He watched the sign of the deer until "Great Spirit" moved the light so he could not see it anymore.

The Sculptor continued with his craft

His father's father chose him to do this. He said he had a dream from the "ancient ones" that he was the "one." His father's father was shown by his father, and it was said that before him, the "ancient ones" showed him. So at a young age, he began. Now that he was in the middle of his life, he was waiting for his dream from the "ancient ones." As he came to this place in his life, he held a position of honor by "Our People" because of this. Our four legged brothers would run from them and they could not be one with them if he did not use his skill. They would not eat if he did not make the piercing stones the right way. They had to strike and enter their brother's body; stopping him without making him suffer with pain.

He continued with a forceful blow to the obsidian core with the granite percussion rock. The "hard hammer" of granite passed most of its energy to the core of the obsidian without absorbing much of the force, and a thin flake was peeled off. He examined the flake and held it to the light. "Great Spirit" was guiding him. He knew it. He next brought out the deer antler "soft hammer" and began the ever delicate shaping of the flake. The soft hammer would absorb much of the energy. When he was young, he was sometimes impatient here and failed because of it. He had learned. As he worked he became excited as he neared its completion. "Great Spirit" was with him! He could tell. This is what his father's father had told him it would look like before he had his dream from the "ancient ones." This one would be the one!

When the Sculptor joined the others, he was pleased to see and smell the meat of his brother, and "Our People" sitting near their fires and he went to them.

That night, the "ancient ones" came to him. He saw his piercing rock and the "ancient ones" held it up to the light and passed it from one to another. He saw his father's father with them and he smiled at The Sculptor. He was now ready, and he was given his dream.

As the warrior slowly stalked the large male mule deer he felt a renewed confidence with the small spear point The Sculptor had bestowed upon him. The Sculptor said he was told in his dream to give it to him, because of all those who hunted, he was most worthy of it. It would bring him and "Our People" good fortune.

The deer tracks were as fresh as they could be with some of the dirt not yet completely settled and he could hear the faint sounds of his prey somewhere just in front of him. He needed to be patient now. He readied his Atl-atl ever so slowly and quietly. The moment when his brother would reveal himself was now near. He waited. His father and others had shown him this when he was very young. This was the most important time to be patient. He now had to listen to his father's lesson. He waited poised. He heard the faint sound of his brother eating the roots of the grass in front of him. The time was close! He could now see his brother's head and part of his chest. He watched his brother's ears searching for him. His brother knew he was nearby. The ears of the mule deer moved away from him and shifted to the other side. He wondered for a moment if one of the other hunters was nearby. He readied himself. He heard the faint familiar sound of one of "Our People" nearby. Only they knew each other's sounds. Hundreds of hunts like this made him recognize them. Even his brother could not tell it was one of "Our People." If he revealed himself to his brother, he could not run forward because of the high rock wall in front of him. "Our People" were to his left. The only escape for him would be toward the valley, but he would not know that until it was too late. He had to find out who had the best chance. He still could not see him fully, but he was prepared to act if he had to. His brother quit eating and stood silent and still: His nostrils sampling the still air surrounding him. His ears pointed toward the rock wall. He was ready to run!

As one of "Our People" to his left silently and quickly stood and revealed himself to our brother and began to release the spear, the great male mountain lion leaped from above him with his vicious jaws open and his razor sharp claws outstretched toward the hunter from the ledge above! The small cascade was prepared for the mule deer, but the warrior instinctively and instantly shifted his aim from the mule deer to the attacking carnivore, now in mid air falling toward his human target. It was released with a force he had not before experienced, and he knew when he completed the arc of his throw, that the cascade would find its mark. The giant beast fell in mid air at the hunter's feet: The lance perfectly imbedded in the center left of his torso just below where his neck joined his chest, and in the great cat's heart.

Our brother would see another day, and so would the hunter.

CHAPTER 5: THE TRAIL RIDE

The smell of the hickory-smoked bacon cooking in Charlie's skillet awakened Alex. She didn't really like to eat it because of its high fat content, but today it would be irresistible. She was hungry. She shouldn't be, after all the calories she had consumed the night before. She would have to do something physical today to burn off some of those calories. She had spent the night on the sofa, but felt rested and fresh. The book she had been reading had slid to the floor sometime during the night, and there was a pillow under her head. Matt must have put it there sometime during the night. The light she had been reading by was turned off. Matt. Always checking on her.

She remembered when she first saw him in the bowling alley lounge nursing a beer with his two buddies in Steubenville, Ohio. It was over thirty-six years ago, but it didn't seem that long. He was a young deputy sheriff in the small Jefferson County department, and she was a newly-licensed registered nurse at the local hospital. As it turned out, one of his buddies attended the same college as she had, and they knew each other. She noticed that Matt and his friend, Bub, were looking her way. After he introduced himself and they talked for a while, she gave him her phone number and they left. Later she told her friend, another nurse, that either she was going to marry him, or someone just like him. They were married eleven months later.

Charlie sounded the metal rebar triangle with the straight rebar section attached by a rawhide string hanging from a nearby pinion pine, signaling that the bacon, eggs, and biscuits were ready to eat. She definitely was going to have to do something physical today. Matt was already up and drinking a cup of coffee with Charlie in front of the camper. Thomas was still asleep in the loft.

She hated to present herself this early to Charlie, or even Matt, without at least brushing her teeth and hair. She did just that, and met them at the picnic table between the camper and the cabin. It was a brisk bright morning in the mountains and the eastern sun was just starting to grace the campsite.

"Looks like a good day for a ride. Charlie says he's ready for a little ass bruisin.'What do think?" Matt announced. Even though Charlie had a lot of natural physical ability, as well as a good seat on a horse, it really wasn't his thing, but today was the exception. Alex would put him on the twenty-year-old quarter horse mare "T." She had a lot of heart, and she would still climb straight up the mountainside if asked. She was still in competition with the other mare "Tequila" to retain the top spot of lead mare, and would not relinquish her position without a quarrel now and then. She would be a good choice for Charlie.

"Sounds good to me. I'll get Tommy up and moving, and we'll head out." Alex said. "Boy that bacon smells good!" And they had their breakfast in the mountain air.

Thomas preferred to have a granola bar and was quick to get ready for the ride. He argued with Alex about brushing his teeth and was anxious to get moving. She had experienced this before with her own children and knew exactly how to handle it. "If you don't want to brush your teeth, it's okay. Did you see old Red's teeth? He doesn't brush them either." Thomas went to brush his teeth.

Alex had wanted to go out west toward the Sylvania range for several days. It had been about a year since they last explored the area on horseback, and they had not yet done it to her satisfaction. It would be a long ride from the ranch, but if they packed a lunch and moved at a good pace, they would be back way before dark, even with the shortened autumn day.

They started south on the old stagecoach road for about three miles and then headed west on a wild burro trail off toward the snow-covered Sierra Nevada, miles off in the distance. It was a site that people would pay thousands of dollars to see. The eastern sun was shining on the snow-capped peaks in the distance and the smell of the pine forest was intoxicating. The horses were full of energy and wanting to run. So they did, and even though he was only nine years old, Thomas handled his Missouri fox trotter Chi Chi as if he were much older. He had been around horses since he was an infant and had no fear. In a way, it was a problem. They were huge animals and passive by nature, but sometimes they were literally "afraid of their own shadows," and they did stupid things. Thomas hadn't been hurt yet, but it would eventually happen. Alex hoped it wouldn't be too bad.

They began to climb and slowed the horses to let them catch their breath. The burro trail began a series of switchbacks as they gained elevation. The cedar and pinion became more plentiful and the evidence of the lightening strikes on them was, too. The air was getting cooler. They had no particular destination in mind, only wanting to see what was on the other side. So they continued. They had been out for about three hours; Charlie seemed to be doing fine and Tommy wasn't complaining. They reached the top of the small mountain and were now at about 8000' elevation, Alex guessed. From there she had an even clearer view of the alpine skyline and the soaring peaks of the Sierra Nevada in the background, as well as a view of the vastness of Death Valley far below her in the foreground. What an inspiring site! It was a good spot for lunch, and probably a good spot for "Woman Looks Down" to check around the area. By now Thomas would probably be hungry, too.

"Hey, what do you guys think about lunch? The horses probably need a break," she offered.

Charlie moaned. "I was waiting for somebody to say something. My butt is killing me."

Thomas snickered, and they dismounted and tied up their mounts. Thomas had to re-tie Charlie's lead line because it was too long and low. "T" might get her legs caught up in all the excess line. "Wow what a view! Look, you can see down into the north end of Death Valley from here," and "Look, you can even see the avalanche chutes over there in California!"

Charlie continued. "This is great!" As Matt got their ham and cheese sandwiches and apples out of the saddlebags, Charlie looked for a good spot to sit and enjoy the view and their lunches. The horses nibbled on the sparse sprouts of mountain grass around them. Matt watched 'Woman Looks Down' walking around the area, looking down and examining the area. She came over to Matt and took her sandwich and apple, and said she was going to look around. 'No surprise here,' Matt thought. The boys found a nice spot where they could all sit on a long fallen log that faced west. It was the perfect spot to enjoy the view. 'Woman Looks Down' wandered off a short way, doing what she did.

She worked her way south from the lunch spot about a hundred yards. She never went much farther away than this from the group when they were out like this. She always tried to be at least within yelling distance, just in case. She then switched directions and headed about fifty yards to the west. The view from there was totally different from where the horses were tied up; she could see another smaller mountain between Death Valley and the Sylvania range. She walked a little more toward the west, and was surprised to find that just before her the ridge gave way to a cliff and a huge vertical drop of several hundred feet. As she continued looking around the area, she saw how the sun played on the shadows on the rocks on the smaller mountain to the west.

Although she was sure she had never been there before, the place had a vague familiarity to it. She continued to walk toward the precipice and stood on a large flat rock. She looked around the area and was excited to see a small deposit of flakes of obsidian lying about. As she dug around in the dirt, she could tell that some of the smaller chips had been worked. This would be a good spot! she thought, and intensified her search. She couldn't take too long or Matt would come looking for her. She poked all around the area picking up pieces of obsidian and chips of other materials. She would have to remember this area, and come back and give it a good look next time. As she walked back out to the flat rock overlooking the high cliff and looked west, she noticed how the shadows on the rock face of the smaller mountain looked like a deer head, complete with antlers. She watched for several minutes, until the light changed and the image disappeared.

"Wo! OO!" "Wo! OO!" Matt called out. She gave him one back, and met him halfway between.

"Did you find anything? You were gone a long time."

"It didn't seem that long. I guess I just got caught up with the view and the whole scene." Alex replied to Matt's question. She looked back at the area again, marking it in her mind.

She would come back.

They continued their ride for about another forty-five minutes, and then decided it was time to head back. It would take several hours to get back, and at this elevation, it was starting to cool off. They headed for the ranch.

Chuck-Wagon Charlie had enough leftovers from the hobo stew to feed the four of them, so he reheated it. His ass was too sore to do any more than that. But it always tasted better on the second day anyway. That night they ate inside the cabin. Charlie brought the "ball" with him and they talked about the day. Alex didn't have a lot to say. Her mind was searching for answers.

The long weekend would be over the following day and they had to head back to Las Vegas. Thomas had to get back to school and Matt and Alex had to get back to work. Charlie had to golf. He was "retired-retired." They would be back in a couple of weeks, or earlier it they could.

"Aren't you forgetting the new arrowhead? You left it on the mantle." Matt asked.

"No, it stays here. It won't ever leave here!" Alex and the masterpiece parted company for the time being.

CHAPTER 6: THE NEW PARTNERS

Red and his new partner spent several days moving Ray's backhoe, Cat, and other equipment down to old Red's camp, so Ray really hadn't had a chance to get out with Red to look over the new claim. He was excited at the idea, as was Red, so they decided take an afternoon and scout the area. They traveled out in Red's old Willeys. The antique four-cylinder workhorse that carried the likes of General Patton around Europe worked just fine for them, and it was dependable, too.

As Red headed north on the county-maintained dirt road and started the assent toward the Palmetto wash, Ray was curious as to how Red found his new spot. Did he look for any unique topographical features, study old claim maps, or read government BLM surveys? It was a mystery and he wanted to know how he did it. So he asked, "Red, how do you figure out where you want to start digging? I mean, you don't just walk around until you get the feeling. How do you do it?"

"You know Ray; I think that's a very interestin' question. When I first started out in this business — it seems like about a hundred years ago — I looked for all the scientific stuff I could find. I studied all the government reports on the valuation of mineral potential from the geologists I could lay my hands on. I studied more assay reports and spent more time in county courthouses than I can remember. I learned everything there is to know about pannin' and rocker and sluice boxes. I tried high bankin' and suction dredgin.' I talked to all the old timers I could find, and even went out with some of them and their little burros. We used shaker tables, mercury and acid and centrifuges to squeeze whatever we could out of a good 'show.' After all of that, I decided one thing. Either you got a nose for it or you don't. So now I cover a lot of ground, poke a lot of holes, and after a while I just sort of know when a 'show' is gonna be a find or not. I guess it's a lot like dousin' for water. Some can do it and some can't."

That's about what Ray thought old Red probably did. He had heard about prospectors just like him. They did exactly what he did and a lot of them hit it big time. In fact, that's how the Comstock and some of the great discoveries by the forty-niners were made. 'Oh well, if that's what worked, what difference did it make how he found it? The important thing was that he did.' Ray considered it all, but he brought his metal detector along with him anyway, just in case old Red's nose wasn't working too well.

As they drove by the Joshua trees and approached the ruins of Palmetto, Red continued talking about all the years he had been prospecting and all the near finds.

Palmetto was another one of those promising communities that had gold and silver at its core. When the metals were gone, so were the people. It was established in 1866 when silver was found and a stamp mill was constructed. It was abandoned later that same year. The locals mistakenly thought that the Joshua trees were related to palm trees, and the name stuck. In 1906 when gold deposits were found, new mines opened and the town swelled to a population of about 200 people. It had a commercial district with stores, saloons, a feed yard, bakeries, a bank, and a doctor's office. By the end of that same year the people started to leave again, and it wasn't too long after that it became the ghost town it now was. Looking around as they passed through it, Ray thought it a shame. The stone buildings that had been constructed to last still stood, but the people didn't. What a wasted effort.

They continued to drive on the county road for about five more miles, winding back and forth as they climbed in elevation. Eventually they came to a less inviting washed out road heading west. It was more of a trail than a road, and in spite of the narrow passageway through the boulders stacked on both sides, still wide enough for the Willeys. Red stopped and shifted old Nellie Bell into four-wheel drive. He turned and smiled a near-toothless smile at Ray and continued to navigate the trail. After about three more miles, the trail all but disappeared, and old Red said, "This is where we start trompin' up the pike." With that, they dismounted the Willeys, and Red headed north with Ray and his metal detector right behind. It wasn't a true trail, with only a few foot tracks leading the way, probably from old Red's comings and goings.

~

He ordered another round of drinks and told another dirty joke. They all laughed until they had tears in their eyes and their sides ached. The alcohol was doing its job.

He had been in Tonopah now for about nine months and he was beginning to feel like he owned the hick town. He could run for mayor and win if he wanted to. "What a bunch of dumbshits," he thought, as he slapped the Esmeralda county official on the back like he was his best and longest-known friend. He didn't know how long it would last, but while it did, he was going to get everything out of these "yahoos" that he could. No matter where he went, he found a never-ending line of potential victims, and every time he did it, he got better at it.

They made it so easy for him. "Why would anyone want to do anything else?" He had learned not to go too fast at first. Just be a nice guy. Have a logical cover story. Don't make anyone jealous. Understate your affluence until you've gained key friendships. Be generous, but not too generous at first. Once you've gotten them on your side, they would vouch for you with the investors. They would do your work. "He's the best thing that ever happened to Tonopah, Nye, and Esmeralda counties," they would say. "Honest? I would trust him with my kids. He was the sole supporter of the kids' softball league. A smart businessman, too! He took those old claims and pumped new life and money into them. He knows how to make money." It was too easy. They would do it all for him. He was gifted!

Later that night, he would give him his early Christmas gift.

Most people, when they thought about Nevada only thought about the glitz of Las Vegas or the action in Reno. Most didn't know it, but Nevada was by far the top gold-producing state in the union with almost seven million ounces of gold harvested just last year alone, which translated into about three billion dollars. The state also was the world's third largest gold producer after the entire countries of South Africa and Australia. Most people didn't know that, but he did, and he was going to make sure his new investors knew it. He would make sure that they knew all about Macsvog International, too, and what a "cutting edge" investment they would be making in his company.

~

"Damn Red. How'd you ever find this place?" They'd been walking uphill for about forty minutes, and although Ray was at least twenty-five years younger than Red, and in fairly good cardiovascular shape, he was winded. Red was amazing! 'The guy had the stamina of a thirty year old!' Ray thought seriously about giving up his unfiltered Pall Malls.

"It's not too much farther, Ray, but we have to climb this here canyon and then take the next fork to the left. We're almost there." Ray wondered still how he ever came upon this place. They stopped for a short breather and rounded a quick bend to the east. Then he could see where Red was working.

"I thought you said you worked up here with the lights on your jeep one night," Ray managed to puff out between gasps.

"I did. We took the shortcut."

~

As he drove his Cadillac Escalade south on the narrow two-lane road called U.S. 95 toward Esmeralda County with his intoxicated public servant seated next to him, they talked about the great potential for wealth in this vast land of opportunity called the U.S.A. They talked about all of the great men of vision and barons of industry who had preceded them when Goldfield and Esmeralda County was the epicenter of the west. They had balls. They were real men. They knew how to get things done. They didn't mind taking a few shortcuts here and there. They had to, in order to get done what needed to get done, for everyone's benefit. So they bent a few dumbass rules every now and then. What counted was results! "I'm talking about men like Tex Richard, Jim Casey, and Charlie Schwab! They were all here back when Goldfield was booming and it was the biggest town in Nevada. You know who they were?"

"I'm not sure, but I heard of 'em," The outclassed public servant mumbled.

"Tex was the builder of Madison Square Garden and Jim

Casey was the founder of U.P.S. Charlie Schwab was the president of U.S. Steel. They were all here! So was Virgil Earp and Jack Dempsey! You think those guys worried about if some bullshit piece of paper was filed in some fuckin' drawer someplace? Hell no! They took care of business! That's what made this country great! They knew how to take care of people, too, and they got shit done!" He could tell the dumb ass was taking it all in as he nodded in the affirmative to everything he was saying.

"Hey, speaking of history, what do you say we stop at the Bunny Tail Ranch for a little action before I drop you off?"

The official groggily responded, "I'd love to, but I didn't bring enough cash."

"Don't worry about it. If a friend can't help another friend out with acquiring a little pussy, then I guess he's not a friend." They both laughed and he banged the dashboard with his fist, delighted with his witty statement, and he told him the story about the Bunny Tail Ranch.

It was one of Nevada's thirty or so legal whorehouses that still operated through out the rural parts of the state. There was also some history to it because it was said that the billionaire Howard Hughes went there frequently back in the early 1960s, and he had a favorite prostitute named Sunny who worked there. In fact, legend has it a garage mechanic named Melvin Dummar found the disoriented eccentric Hughes not far from the brothel lying alongside the road, and he left his entire fortune to Dummar in what was known as the controversial Mormon Will.

"Now that's a story I've heard about! If it's good enough for Howard Hughes, then I guess it's good enough for me. Hey, if you're the one payin,' then I'm the one layin'." He laughed as if he were the featured comedian on the David Letterman Show. The married-with-three-children intoxicated public official walked into the famed whorehouse with his new partner's left arm around his shoulder, ready to receive his early Christmas gift. It was too easy.

~

As Red and Raymond approached the new 'show,' Ray saw the vehicle tracks and how Red entered the site with his truck and jeep from the north side. He looked for any markers of the claim around the area, but didn't see them. It was evident that Red had some sort of method to working the area by the pattern of disruptions in the mountain soil.

"Hey Red. I been luggin' this apparatus around for about and hour. Do you mind if I sniff around with it a little?"

"Hell no! I told you we was partners. Go ahead!" With that, Ray turned on his Fisher Gold Bug 11 metal detector with the automax v4 pinpointer probe and 10" elliptical searchcoil and began sweeping the eluvial hillside. It took a little while to tune it to the unique properties of the area he was scanning. Once he did, he hooked up the earphones to the device so he could better hear the nuances of the sounds it produced.

Within an hour and-a-half, Red and Raymond had recovered three small nuggets about the size of a match head, and a much larger one buried just beneath the surface at about eighteen inches.

See I told you this was gonna be a good show! The taller Red placed his left arm around the shoulder of his new partner. He did a little hop, and then slapped Ray on the back. It was a good day!

CHAPTER 7: SPRINGTIME

Even though it was early March and there was still a lot of snow on the ground, the migrating red-tailed hawks had already taken up residence in their perennial nest in the towering Cottonwood tree next to the spring and were getting an early start. They had come back to the same spot now for the last three years to breed and raise their young. It made perfect sense. Everything they needed in order to thrive was right there.

The mountainous area had received more than its normal share of snowfall the past winter, but it was a welcome site. Magruder Mountain and the Sylvania range had not been in a true drought, but it had been fairly dry the past several years. The ever-present threat of forest fires was always a concern, and the more precipitation this area got, the less of a threat it became. The drifting snow had blocked the area where the old stagecoach road intersected with state route 266 and Matt and Alex had not been able to get to the cabin since the last part of January because of it. They were both anxious for spring to come and they missed their time together at the ranch. It had been a trying couple of months for Matt at the casino with the slot department investigation, and he was ready for a break. Alex was tired of the pace at work, too, and couldn't wait to tramp around the ranch again.

~

When the accounting department had found an abnormally large variance in the slot department's "hold," they notified Matt and the general manager that they believed something was wrong. As Matt reviewed the payout records, he found that on one night, two slot machines had paid out almost $200,000 in $100 coupons, all within a half-hour time span. Something was wrong. He went to work.

After reviewing the video surveillance of the area where the two machines were located, he didn't observe anything unusual. No abnormal activity was noted. Regular players entertaining themselves. Slot employees going about their usual activities. Slot technicians attending to their duties. In fact the two machines in question didn't attract any undue attention at all. "You would think that kind of a pay out would attract some sort of attention." He decided to follow the money, and began tracing the cash payouts of the coupons from the bill validator kiosks. He began to review video coverage of the kiosks at about the times the records showed some of the questionable coupons were cashed. He zeroed in on a slightly built older Asian male and backtracked his movements throughout the casino with the video coverage. He definitely was a suspect and had cashed at least $9000 of the known $100 coupons at different kiosks around the casino. Matt's attention was now focused on him. He wasn't the total answer to what was going on, but he was part of it. Matt was sure he was on to something. At one point, Matt thought he saw the suspect hand a players card to one of the Pai Gow poker dealers just before playing, and then it was handed back to him. The video showed the time of 12:41 a.m. If the dealer swiped the card, then maybe there would be some information contained in their computer records about his identity. At 12:41 a.m. at Pai Gow table six, the records revealed that club card member Huang Woo bought into the game for three hundred dollars. He played for about ten minutes and then left. He listed his residence as 1428 Fisher

Street, Vancouver, British Columbia.

Matt continued to backtrack with the video recordings throughout the casino attempting to follow the whereabouts of Woo. At 1:03 a.m. he was recorded getting into a cab at valet. The cab number was 409. Matt contacted the Taxicab Authority and asked for the cab's records at around that time frame. "Sorry, sir, we can only release those records to a law enforcement agency or by subpoena," the bureaucrat said.

"Damn! I was on a roll," he said to himself. He wouldn't let that stop him. "Hey, John, do you still know anyone over at the TA?" John Casey had retired from the Bureau about two years before Matt and had taken over the agency before he moved on to the Federal Transportation Security Administration at McCarran Airport.

"Yea, the guy who replaced me. I recommended him for the job. What do you need?"

Records showed that Woo was dropped off at Caesars Palace at 1:18 a.m. "Hey Bruce, it's Matt; can you check something out for me?"

"Sure, what you got?" Bruce Yearington had retired from the Bureau the same year as did Matt, and for a brief time they worked together on the public corruption squad. Like Matt, he was now the director of security at the casino. Matt filled him in.

"Yep. He stayed here for three days. We've got his address and phone number. Looks like he's from Vancouver."

"Great! One more thing; can you pull his room folio and see if he made any phone calls from his room?"

"Yeah, he did: two to Vancouver and one to a local number. The local number looks like it might be a cell phone."

"Thanks a million. If you need anything, let me know."

"Jenine, will you contact PBX and run this phone number in their data base and see what we've got?" Jenine was Matt's data specialist and she had earned her keep more than once in situations just like this.

"Bingo! It looks like this number is assigned to one of our slot technicians. I already checked with HR. He's been here for about ten years, and he's never had any problems."

When it was all over, the technician rolled over on three other employees and gave up six of the Asian organized crime group members. In return for his cooperation, he would get a reduced prison sentence. The others wouldn't do so well. It was the same old story. They had gotten greedy. They had figured out a way to manipulate the machine payouts by using a "looping device" and diverting the signals to a remote location in the slot tech's workshop, where the coupons were printed out. If they had just not gotten greedy, there was no telling how long they could have gotten away with the scheme.

It was time to get out of town for a couple of days.

~

Even though the spring thaw was ongoing, there remained a couple of high snow drifts on the stagecoach road, but if he got a run for it in four wheel drive, Matt was pretty sure he would be able to push on through. "Hold on Alex, I'm going to hit this drift a little faster than I should. We'll be through it in a second." Alex braced herself, and was surprised to find that it wasn't as bad as she thought it would be. They were now on almost solid ground, although it was muddy. They would probably have to park down by the corrals and carry their supplies up to the cabin. It was only about a quarter of a mile, but it was narrow and had several sharp turns in it. The snow had drifted several feet into the cabin road in some places, so they would have to hike it. She felt like she needed the exercise anyway after the three-and-a-half hour drive. They decided to leave the horses back in Las Vegas this trip. The road conditions up were too uncertain this time of year, and the horses were spoiled anyway with the mild winter in Las Vegas. Alex liked to spoil them like this. It's why she brought them up in the summer, so she could spoil them.

~

"Look, the hawks are back." Alex called to Matt. "It's good to see them again. I guess that's a real sign that spring has sprung." They watched them flutter about the old nest setting up house. They would enjoy seeing them and their offspring throughout the spring, summer, and early fall. Within several weeks, the mature hawks would once again accept Matt and Alex as part of the landscape and wouldn't object to their presence so much. Right now, they were fairly vocal about them interrupting their peace and quiet, but that would change.

Alex had been looking forward to this trip, even if it was just for a long weekend. It had been too long since she had been up here, and she needed the solitude. She was looking forward to just relaxing, doing some reading, and spending some quality time with Matt. This was good for them.

Alex was always nervous when they opened the cabin door for the first time each season. She always half expected to see the worst and the worst for her would be to see that some rodent had gotten in and crapped all over the place. She would have to clean everything from top to bottom if that was the case. As Matt opened the door, she held her breath … no sign of any pack rats! "All right!" She was good to go. Matt knew what her fear was, and one time he put a realistic-looking rubber rat on the kitchen table before they left that weekend. Her reaction when then came back the next week, while funny for him, caused her a lot of anxiety for a few minutes, and he paid the price for the next hour and-a-half. It wasn't worth it.

The second thing she did was look over at the fireplace mantle to make sure that her masterpiece was still in its place of prominence centered in the display case. It was and it was looking right at her. "Good," she thought and started to unpack for the weekend. Matt went out on the covered porch and brought in some firewood for the fireplace. Before long, they had a roaring fire going and some of the winter chill was beginning to fade. After dinner, they each had a glass of old Red's peach brandy that he had given them the last time they saw him. It was all very soothing; just what they needed. It was almost dark and the night was going to be clear. The stars up there looked like they were so close you could almost touch them, and so many of them, too. Even though it was cold out, they would have to go out on the porch before bed and look at the night sky.

In the morning, Matt would try to get over to Red's place and check in on him. He was sure that Red and Ray hadn't been able to do much prospecting the last couple of months because of the weather, so Red was probably spending a lot of time by himself. Since they joined up last fall, they had made a lot of progress with Ray's equipment and their production was increasing every week. They were actually making some money.

They decided to go to bed, and get an early start on the day tomorrow.

That night as she slept, the mute relic spoke to her again for the second time.

The legend of the spearhead and how the great hunter killed the giant cat carried on for many years. The story grew with each passing generation until it took on a mystical status. Some said the stone implement was forged by Great Spirit himself, and whoever possessed it would have great power beyond this world. He would be able to look into the next world and would have this world do his bidding. Just as the great hunter who first received it, the one who possessed it had to be worthy of it. Whatever happened to the powerful spearpoint? No one person knew. Some said that Great Spirit took it back, because he could not find anyone worthy of its power again. Someday he would, and then he would give it back.

When he was very young, before he could think of many things, he would listen to his father Ta'vibo talk with Wadziwob and others. "The earth will swallow the whites up, and all of our dead who are in the other world will be among us again. There will be happiness and no hunger." He would remember watching them do the dancing, calling for them. They did this many times. He still could remember this.

When he was still very young, his father and then his mother went to the other world, and he went to live with the whites named Wilson not far from where they did the dancing. His name now would be Jack Wilson. He had to work, but the whites were good to him, and he liked their Jesus. He liked the way they said that Jesus went to the other world too, and then came back. He liked the message of happiness for all. It was like his father's message about the other side, but Jesus was white. Maybe there were two other worlds: one for whites and one for Our People. But the Wilsons said the white Jesus was for all people. Maybe the whites would not be swallowed up by the earth. He hoped that the Wilsons would not. He would pray to their Jesus, and ask him to spare the Wilsons. He would do the dance that he remembered to make it not happen like this.

Many whites were coming to Our People's land now, and Jack Wilson was now a man. Great Spirit and Jesus had listened to him because the Wilsons lived a long time and they had not been swallowed up by the earth. They went to the other world when he was at the beginning of being a man. He did the dance for them and others after they were gone. He was no longer Jack Wilson. Now, he was a woodcutter, and his name was Wovoka.

As he sat in the shade along the base of the soft volcanic white boulder, he carved the story of the hunt for sheep and deer, and how coyote tricked the snakes into scaring them off, while he ate the pinion nuts and drank the cool water from the ground.

He then went back to work and started to cut the pinions that were done with their lives. It was forbidden by Great Spirit to cut the living ones, because they gave them nuts when there was no meat. When he started to drag out a limb, he saw a beautiful spearhead that one of his brothers had left behind or lost. He picked it up.

His head ached as if a wild horse had stepped on it and it turned into night, and then it turned into day, but a different color of day. He fell to the ground. He felt like he could not move, and he saw people he knew who were in the other world. He saw his mother and his father and others. It was not a place of sorrow. There were lots of deer and rabbits. There was happiness. He was given a vision, and told about things that others did not know. He was told that someday those who were in the other world would rise up and be in this world again. It would be a different world: a better world. There would be no hunger or unhappiness. He was told to not lie. Not to harm others, and to work for the whites, if they paid him. He was shown how to do the dance and given instructions to make it so. He would be given powers that others did not have. The dance must be done in a special way, in a sacred place; a place like this place.

Some would call Wovoka the Messiah, and later on, others would call him "Grandfather." The first ghost dance would be done here, at this place.

The word of Wovoka's revelation of hope spread throughout the Great Basin and to the Great Plains. Shaman and great leaders of nations came from as far away as the Lakota Souix and Arapaho nations to hear his message and learn of the ghost dance, and its message. They were eager for a revelation. Many like the Big Foot band of the Lakota Sioux added to the message and believed they could become invincible to the whites' bullets. White people heard about the ghost dance and thought it was meant to drive them out and hurt them. They were afraid of the movement and misunderstood it. It was forbidden by the government, because it caused unrest among whites and Our People.

When the U.S. 7th Cavalry contingent of 500 troops, supported by four Hotchkiss artillery guns, surrounded the encampment of the Miniconjou Sioux because they had been performing the sacred dance, it soon got out of hand.

When Wovoka heard about the 146 men, women, and children, as well as the twenty-five soldiers who had died at Wounded Knee, he felt overwhelming guilt and went into the Sylvania Mountains for six months. No one saw him and many believed he had gone to the other world because of his self-inflicted shame.

After many painful months, Wovoka knew that the vision given him was a different vision from what his Sioux brothers wanted it to be. His was a message of hope and happiness: One of reunion and unification. It was not one of confrontation and vanquishment. It was about peace and tolerance. He finally had peace. His message was not heard of anymore.

After many years, he went back to the great white boulder where he told the story on the rock a long time ago, and put the spearpoint back where he found it. Now he was old, and springtime would be coming soon.

~

"Are you going to be able to get over to Red's?"

"I don't think I can get there on the back road with all the snow. I'll have to go out onto the main road and take the road to the south off of 266 to get there. If it's too bad, I'll park and hoof it on in. It's only about a mile. It shouldn't be a problem."

Alex gave him a light kiss on the cheek, and handed him the loaf of homemade nut bread wrapped in aluminum foil. It was her grandmother's recipe that she had inherited from her. She made her first loaf with Granny's help over fifty years ago when she was just a little girl, and still kept the family baking tradition alive. With that, Matt started out to Red's place. There were now snow ruts on the stagecoach road from the F350 the day before, so Matt got into the ruts and followed them down to the main road. As he got to the turnoff to Red's place, he saw that there were old vehicle tracks on the road going towards Red's place, but the recent snow had partially covered them. There wasn't anything fresh leading in or out. He noticed, however, that there were fresh tire tracks at the entrance, as if someone started to enter the road, and then thought better of it.

They looked like they might be a couple of days old. No foot tracks were noted. Maybe Ray tried to stop by and decided to return later.

It didn't look like there were any large drifts ahead, so Matt put it in four-wheel drive and headed south through the snow. The going was easier because the sun struck the road more directly here than at Pigeon Spring, and much more of the white stuff had melted. The ground was still somewhat solid, so the mud was not a big issue. He approached the open gate to Red's place and was happy to see Red coming out of the trailer; they waved to each other. Red must have heard him coming up the road. Maybe his hearing was improving, but it was probably just a coincidence.

"Hey Matt. It's good to see you. I was wonderin' when you and Alex might be back up. Did she come up with you?" He was grinning his almost toothless smile, happy to see his friend.

"She sure did. She's up at the cabin, and she told me to tell you hi. I have strict instructions to make sure you get this," and he handed him the loaf of Granny's nut bread.

You would have thought he just won a million bucks on the crap table from his reaction to the minor gift. "Oh man! If it's what I think it is, you made my day! Hell you made my month! It's that nut bread she makes, ain't it?"

"You guessed it right. She said you liked it so much the last time we saw you at our place, she was going to make you a loaf the next time we came up."

"Hey come on in. I got some coffee heated up from yesterday, and it's still not ruined yet. It'll go good with this here nut bread." The tall old redhead had to duck down when he entered through the small trailer door entrance. Matt carefully registered Red's comments, even the little hop Red did when he took it, so he could tell Alex how much he appreciated her small gift.

Red kept his humble surroundings surprisingly neat, considering his "hermit like" status. "Has Ray been around? I know with all of the snow, you guys probably haven't been able to work the claim much."

"You're right about that, we haven't been up there for about three weeks. This last storm put us out of business for a while. I think spring's just about here, so we should be gettin' back to it real soon."

As Matt looked around the trailer, he saw an old black-and-white framed photo sitting on the shelf behind his bed of a much younger Red with a beautiful, petite, dark-haired woman, probably in her early thirties, holding a baby. Red had a full head of teeth in the photo and was grinning at the camera. He had his arm around her shoulder, and from the period of dress, Matt guessed the photo was taken sometime in the early sixties or maybe the late fifties. Matt guessed the baby in the picture was his son little Red from Fresno. He never talked about a wife, and Matt wondered if the young woman in the picture had anything to do with why he lived the way he did. He wouldn't push it. If old Red wanted to talk about her, then he would. Matt stayed away from the subject.

"Last week I drove over to Fresno and spent a couple of days with little Red. He's gettin' divorced and doesn't want it. He's havin' a rough time of it. Said he's gonna be spendin' a lot more time over here helpin' Ray and me this summer. Sometimes life is hard on some people." Matt could see the hurt in Red's old eyes.

"Since we've had this snow and things are slow, Ray's been tryin' to get all of our paperwork for the claim done. You know

I never did any of that paperwork stuff, but Ray says since this looks like this could be a serious 'show,' we better get our papers in order. It takes a lot filin' forms with the county, the BLM, and surveys and whatnot. Plus, he wants to make R&R Mining official with the proper papers and all."

"I'm sure it's the right thing to do. You guys have to protect your interests."

After a refill of the day-old coffee and a slice of the nut bread, Matt and Red said their goodbyes. "I'll see you in a couple of weeks. Be careful," and Matt headed out toward the main road. When he got to the paved 266, he turned east and headed up the mountain toward Pigeon Spring. As he got about a quarter of a mile past the turnoff to Red's place, he saw a black Cadillac SUV heading west toward him. It neared him and Matt couldn't resist his old SOG habit of trying to read the license plate before the vehicle passed by: NOLES. Matt could see in the rearview mirror that the vehicle's brake lights briefly came on and off as the driver approached the turnoff to Red's place, but he kept on heading west toward Fish Lake Valley.

NOLES. That's what he thought he saw on the personalized front plate of the car, but maybe he was mistaken.

~

"How was Red? Did you give him Granny's nut bread?" He thought it respectful that even though she was the one who made it from scratch, and her sweet Granny had been gone for about thirty years, it was still "Granny's" nut bread. He wondered if his kids would still call it that after Alex was gone.

"You would have thought he hit the jackpot," and Matt gave her a blow-by-blow description of the presentation of her small, but very appreciated gift. "Looks like you've been playing in the snow." He noticed her snow-covered boots on the cabin deck, and her damp wranglers.

"I took a walk up past the spring. Did you know there's a petroglyph up on the back side of that giant white boulder across from the spring?"

CHAPTER 8: THE INVESTORS

"Macsvog International; how may I help you? Mr. Sandefur isn't in right now; he's in a meeting. May I take a message?" She gave the caller the standard response that Mr. Sandefur had instructed, unless it was someone from the list that he had provided her with. She was starting to get more familiar with the names on the list, and almost had them all memorized. She couldn't believe she landed the job out of all of the others that he had interviewed. She had gone to the community college in Carson City and received her associate degree in business administration, and it had immediately paid off. Mr. Sandefur said that of all the candidates who interviewed for the position, he was most impressed with her communication skills and the fact that she had gone to the trouble of earning a degree. He was a great boss, and she couldn't believe that she had gotten so lucky. If everything went well, she was going to buy her first new car! He was really a wonderful man.

On the phone with the elderly man from Wheeling, West Virginia, he talked about the assay reports and the core samples he would provide. "It's all certified and backed by the assets in the holding company. While it isn't as secure, of course, as a government bond or something that is insured by the FDIC, the rate of return on the short-term investment of fifty thousand and above has been averaging 75 to 80 percent within a year. Some have done even better than that. What with the skyrocketing price of the gold market lately, I wouldn't be surprised if it went higher than that within the next six months.

Of course, Macsvog International will only be offering this opportunity on a limited basis. The board of directors is considering buying back some of the stock because of the tremendous success we have had, and we are considering other capital ventures. I can send you all of the necessary forms you will need in order to get you started, or you can go to our website and print them out for yourself. While you are on the website, take a couple of minutes and look at some of the great things we have been doing. Remember, I'm not sure how long this will be available, so once you have made your decision, it's important to act quickly. I'm not supposed to tell anyone that, but you remind me a lot of my uncle Robert. He worked for a coal mining company near Morgantown. That's around your area, isn't? He was a member of the local UMW back years ago. Thanks for calling, and I look forward to working with you."

Another dumbshit just took the bait. That Morgantown thing and his "Uncle Robert" was a nice touch. He knew about Morgantown, because he had served about nine months at the minimum security Federal Correction Institution there about fifteen years ago, and his "roommate" was a former UMW official named Robert something, who was caught taking bribes. "Kiel, my man, you are too good," he mumbled, and he went back to his porno website. Kiel. That was smoke and mirrors, too.

"Mr. Sandefur, before I leave for the day, do you want me to Federal Express those dividend checks to the investors? I think there are about thirty of them for this month. If I get them out today, they will receive them before the first of next month."

"Oh, I'm glad you reminded me of that, Dawn. Just make sure that the fund statements are in with the checks. Thanks a lot, and I'll see you tomorrow." It was all part of the scam. You get fifty to a hundred grand out of them, or more if you can, and then start sending them a little bit back, month by month. It had to look like their investment was paying off big. He would pay off one or two of the smaller investors just as he promised, and then they would put their whole life savings in with him or vouch for Macsvog International with other dumbshits. The greedy fucks.

~

Filing the articles of incorporation and the accompanying paperwork was not an easy thing to do, even with the help of the online service Ray had retained. R&R Mining would be a limited liability company. It required a Company Data Sheet, Articles of Organization, and an Operating Agreement. It was necessary to have a Waiver of Notice of Election of Officers, even if it was only old Red and himself. They had to get approval of the form of Certificate of Ownership and Authorization of Banking arrangements. A Wavier of Notice and an Election of Manager for the upcoming year had to be filed. They had to set up accounting records and address the Dissolution Event and Buy/Sell Events. All of this paperwork had to be filed with the Secretary of State and with the Esmeralda County Clerks Office, and it all had to be notarized by a Notary Public. After about five weeks, Ray thought he had it just about ready to go.

~

As the clerk block-stamped the various applications and petitions that came into the courthouse, he was on the lookout for those that might be of interest to Kiel Sandefur. After all, they were "best friends," and Kiel was right about those rich guys from a long time ago. They really did know how to get things done, and it was for the overall good of the community. Kiel was a smart guy, and he knew what he was talking about. He should know about things before anybody else did. Kiel was a lot like that Madison Square Garden guy he talked about at the whorehouse. And he did pay off his MasterCard after Christmas for him. What a relief that was! It was great to have a friend like Kiel.

"Red, you wouldn't believe all the hoops I had to jump through just to get us incorporated. I had to file this paper and that paper and more forms because of those forms. But I think we got it all done. As soon as we get the receipt back from the Secretary of State, we will be officially R&R Mining. Once we get that, then we can get the claim filed. I've been doing a lot of checking up on that process, and it's about as mixed up as a four-peckered owl. That's the big thing though. We have to get it all done right, so we can protect ourselves. I think this operation is gonna go big time!" They had another sip of the peach brandy. Ray was becoming a convert.

~

"Hey Kiel, I think I might have something for you. I haven't recorded the file yet. I'll wait until you get a chance to look it over. How about we get together up in Tonopah tonight for a drink. I'll see you at the Mizpah in the bar around six o'clock."

CHAPTER 9: BACK TO WORK

"Listen, I don't know exactly what they are up to, but I'll be following this behind the scenes. If they are on to something good, they'll have to file an unpatented claim if it's on government land, which it probably is. Ninety-five percent of Nevada is. It's always faster to file it with the county first because of all of the bullshit paperwork with the BLM. They still have to file with the Feds, but whoever files first, no matter at what level of government it is, has the rights to the claim. Go ahead and record the Articles of Incorporation just like you're supposed to, and watch for any unpatented claim filings. I'll bet these yahoos know at least that much, so they'll probably file with the county first. You did good! Let's go to work." He palmed him five one-hundred-dollars bills. "You got time for the Bunny Tail tonight?"

~

Charlie and his wife Gloria checked into the hotel room under the name of Mr. and Mrs. Charles Meister. It was one of his cover names he used when he and the SOG team were working covert operations. He still had the state-issued drivers license in the name and it was valid for five more years. He would have to figure out some way to get another one when this one expired if it he needed to. He and Gloria looked exactly like the couple that he wanted them to look like: older fifties, a little paunch on the mid-sections, here for a quiet weekend. Maybe they would take in a couple of shows and have a nice meal or two at one of the many fine restaurants. Charlie met up with Matt a few minutes later at a gas station one block west of the casino and talked. It was all smoke and mirrors.

"Make sure you photograph where you plant the money, and keep a log of when you entered the rooms. I want to make sure that when we do the lock interrogation, it's fairly close to the times reflected in your log."

"I find this all very insulting. After all, I am Mr. Meister." He indignantly responded to Matt's instructions, half-grinning.

"Here are the other nine keys for one room on each floor. All of the cleaning people are assigned to one floor in groups. I didn't want them to see you going into different rooms on the same floor. It might look a little suspicious otherwise. You don't have to take ten showers in all the rooms, but trash them up, like you've been spending some time in them. Put some clothing in the drawers and leave some bathroom stuff out. Maybe even leave some cash in an opened room safe when you go out for the day. I've got a couple of IPODS from Lost and Found that were never claimed. They seem to come up missing a lot, too. Record the denominations and serial numbers of the cash you leave in the rooms. If we get lucky, we might be able to catch some of them with the money on them. That makes it a slam-dunk. Charge everything to the room. If you need to see me, I'll meet you here. Otherwise, call me on the cell phone. Good luck! And above all else, have fun, and tell Gloria I said hi."

"Aye Aye, Captain. See you around." Charlie and Matt separated company.

Matt monitored trends in the giant hotel-casino complex, and when he saw that an inordinate number of guest incident complaints were coming in one area, he employed counter measures, like the sting Charlie and Gloria were now doing. It wasn't always easy to tell if a guest's complaint about missing items or other matters were legitimate or not. In this business, there were a lot of other factors to consider. Did the husband lose all of his money gambling and was afraid to tell his wife, so he created a phony thief? Was the car really stolen from the parking lot or was it an insurance job? Did the guest really slip and fall on the water left on the walkway floor, or was he going for the deep pockets? Even though the guest's wallet was stolen by a hooker and security had her in custody, the victim didn't want to file a complaint with the police, because his wife back in Omaha might find out. Did the guest really find a piece of plastic in his mashed potatoes, or did he just want a free meal? All of these matters needed to be considered.

The most difficult part of figuring these things out was to do it without insulting the legitimate guests, and start losing business because of it. By its very nature, sometimes one would slip by you. It was not the normal black-and-white world of law enforcement that he was used to. There were a lot of gray areas in this business, and lots of shades of that color, too. There were different rules for different people, too. Matt had learned to check on a person's play or who the person knew before he was 86'd from the property, or before he made any decision about what course of action he was going to take. He had also learned not to judge a book by its cover. There were a lot of Howard Hughes types still hanging around Las Vegas. It was all very interesting work, and he enjoyed the challenges presented by the complex color called gray.

As "Mr. Meister" worked his way throughout the hotel setting up the rooms, photographing, and planting cash and other valuables, he thought about a couple of other times Matt called on Mr. Meister's assistance. He wondered why he did it.

He concluded that it was the closest thing to Matt's former employment that he could legally participate in and he still enjoyed getting the bad guys. But sometimes Matt's assignments were over the top.

"Listen, Charlie. I know it sounds weird, but I really think this guy could be dangerous. He used to work in one of the restaurants before I got here, and he had some beef with a couple of employees. He was always talking about shooting people, and they fired him and 86'd him from the property. I heard from a reliable source that he has been coming back in during the late evening hours on swing shift."

"So why don't you just arrest him for trespass or just kick him out again?"

"Well, here's the thing. My informant says that he is now on his way to becoming a she and has had the hormone treatments. He just hasn't had the unit removed yet."

"It's all very interesting, but why are you telling me this?"

"When he was here the last time, he was making a lot of inquiries about the employee who he thinks was responsible for him losing his job.

"I'm still in the dark. What's this got to do with me?"

"Well, because he is dressed like a woman now, and none of the other employees recognize him, so he thinks he can come in safely." Matt said the next part real fast. "He's working as a prostitute at one of the bars in the casino, and I want you to get picked up by him so we can bust him."

Before Charlie knew it he was sitting next to the guy, talking about going up to the room for a little action.

"Remember, the cops want you to get the specific proposition on what type of sexual act he's willing to perform up in the room and an agreement on a price before they will accept our affidavit for the arrest. So once that's done, call my office extension like you are ordering a bottle of wine from room service. When I get the call, we'll hit the room and make the arrest."

"Hello room service. I'd like to order a nice bottle of Merlot please."

"I'm sorry, pal, this ain't room service." The gruff voice on the other end responded.

"Sure this is room service. This is extension 6240, isn't it?" The male hooker was starting to rub Charlie's neck.

"Look pal. I told you, this ain't room service," and he hung up.

"Why don't we get started? It might be a while before the wine gets here."

"No, I think I need a drink first, if you don't mind." That son of a bitch, Matt, he thought. Just then there was a knock on the door. "Room Service." He didn't know why he put up with it.

~

"Let's take a ride up to the claim if you think we can make it. I think we should at least start putting the boundary markers in."

"I don't know, Ray. It seems to me that it's just like we're showin' our hand. There's some sneaky bastards still around these parts. That's why I never did put nothin'up when I was on my own. Course I never had a partner neither, cept' lil'Red, and we never did do anything in a big way."

"I know what you mean, Red, but I been reading up on this stuff and the law says that the first step is to locate your monument. That's what they call the boundary markers of the claim. Once that's done, we have ninety days to file with the

BLM and the county. The claim still has to be filed with both agencies within the ninety days, but the county process is quicker. Now if one of those sneaky bastards gets wind about the claim in the meantime, the law sides with the ones who put up the monument first, and that's us. But you're right, it's like we're putting up a sign saying, "Gold mine here, come and help yourselves."

"I guess it's like one of those catch twenty-two things, ain't it?" By that, Red signaled he understood.

The old Jeep didn't have a top on it and of course no heater either, but they were fairly well-dressed for the weather. It was clear and sunny, but cold. The old work-horse made its way through the Palmetto ruins without any trouble, and they followed some old ATV tracks on the winding county road. Red had it in four-wheel drive ever since they left the paved route 266, and a lot of the snow had melted because of the latitude and the way the sun struck the south-facing foothill. So far, so good. As they made their way toward the rougher trail turn off, the road held up, but it was doubtful they could traverse the narrower shortcut. "Maybe we should take the long way. It might be easier." Ray offered. Knowing that, if by chance, they did make it through on the "shortcut" road, they still would have to hoof it through the snow on foot, and he didn't want the old man showing him up again. He still hadn't given up the Pall Malls.

Old Red gave him that same old toothless smile that said, "I know what you were thinking." He let him off the hook, with a mere, "You're probably right." Surprisingly, the rest of the way went without a hitch.

"I think in another few days we can get up here and start working this spot again. What do think, Red?"

"It sure looks a lot better than I thought it would. I say let's get goin'. I got a real good feelin' about this show."

They spent the rest of the day walking the area and placing the four-foot markers on the boundary of their claim. In some spots the ground was still frozen, so they had to use a matic pick to get the job done. As he was digging the hole for the marker for the center of the claim near the spot he had originally been working, Red said, "Looky here, Ray. I found an old ivory button here just under the dirt. Those old timers didn't leave a rock unturned, did they?"

"We better be getting back, Red. It's getting late, and I don't think we had better be driving around here after dark this time of year." They headed back to Red's, excited about getting back to some serious work. They talked about their different theories on how deep the vein might run, if there even was one, and what the direction of their efforts should be. Now Raymond was getting the fever, and Red fed it with his tale of the lost mine and the story of the richest vein since the Comstock that was around these parts someplace, but never re-discovered.

"Yep! They say it's around here somewheres, but ain't nobody ever been able to find it. Back when Goldfield was the center of everything in the early nineteen hunderts, the story goes that some old mean drunk named Wallace Stow stumbled across it when he was between drunks, and doin' what everyone else was doin' them days: prospectin'. He's sposed to brought into one of the assayers the purest and biggest chunk of gold Esmeralda County ever saw. Story goes, that same night, he went down to the Eureka Saloon and got on a good and mean drunk. He started braggin' about how he was gonna be able to buy the town ten times over now that he was rich. Somebody had seen him about a month earlier down at a little tent saloon that was operatin' over there at the Pigeon Spring stamp mill, so everybody knew his new 'show' was around those parts somewheres. Granted it's a big area from Macgruder Mountain to Palmetto and the Sylvania Mountain range, but everyone knew it was around these parts, but nobody 'cept the old mean drunk Stow knew exactly where. The story goes that he got real drunk that night, drunker than he usually got, and tried to rape one of the whores. When the sheriff broke into the room 'cause she was yellin' bloody murder; he had a knife to her throat. Virgil Earp had done some work as a deputy for the sheriff, and the sheriff had learned Earp's technique of calmly walkin' up to what ever son of a bitch was causin' trouble and hittin' him upside the head with a blackjack real quick like. He knocked the mean bastard out, and took him to jail to wait for trial. When they come to feed him in the morning, he was found dead layin' on the jailhouse bed. Seems he choked to death that night on his own puke. A proper death for the mean bastard I would say. Now everybody in Goldfield was out tryin' to figure where his claim was. Some said he probably jumped somebody else and stole the sample he brought in for assayin.' Others swore he had a claim out here somewhere. Anyways, far as anyone knows, it's still waitin' to be re-found."

"Well, Red, that's quite a story. You know what I think? I think it's all a bunch of malarkey. It's like Big Foot and UFOs. It's all "plastic bananas." That's what I think."

And he winked and smiled at his partner, Red. He hoped he was wrong.

~

The smart-ass young doctor had just hung up with Alex, who was now wondering how a mere nurse knew that the treatment plan that he had discussed was replete with major flaws. After all he was the surgeon, and what did she know about it? She was just a nurse. It was supposed to be a formality. He had to get the medical case manager RN to concur before the insurance carrier would authorize the surgery. Usually, it wasn't a problem. He would just call in and discuss his plan and tell the RN why there was a medical necessity to do the back surgery. He usually talked in a very authoritative tone and because he was the doctor, and the person on the other end of the phone was only a nurse, he always got what he wanted. This one was a real bitch! She questioned his reason for the necessity of the surgery!

"I understand that you want to do the fusion on L4, L5, and I'm certainly not questioning the surgical necessity. I just believe that it's premature to do such an invasive procedure at this point. Prior to this last injury, he was responding positively to the intensive physical therapy. My concern with this patient is that I believe he has a high risk for arachnoiditis, and before he undergoes back surgery, I would like to see him continue with the physical therapy." She had seen way too many surgeons too eager do what they got paid for, cutting people, and had witnessed the sad results of too many bungled jobs, especially in the nerve-laden interchanges that back surgeries involved. In her experience, most people got substantially better after three or four years with therapy alone.

The bitch did have one small point though. He had to give her that. If he did the proposed spinal surgery and the morphogenic bone graft, there was always the risk of arachnoiditis scar tissue.

CHAPTER 10: THE HOLIDAY WEEKEND

R&R Mining was now a real outfit and they even had the paperwork from the Nevada Secretary of State's office to prove it. Red and Raymond were now in full swing and they had decided to follow the gold flakes and nuggets wherever they led them. In this case, they were being led deeper into the ground and they were chasing a promising show. They found other evidence, besides the ivory button, that someone before them had been working in this area. There wasn't much evidence, but it was clear. The small volcanic natural indentation in the hillside had accumulated debris from a small flood many years before, and a lush creosote bush flourished in the protected spot. It hid the evidence of the beginnings of some prospector's earlier efforts, but stopped short of the full-blown excavation that you would normally see. No supporting timbers or makeshift rock foundation of a rough living quarters were around the area. Nor were there the telltale signs of the trash they always left behind, like the old rusted-out tin cans and ever-present broken whiskey bottles. If they were alive today, it would probably be safe to say that the old prospectors would not be card-carrying members of the Sierra Club. Maybe the Spaniards or the Chinese started working the spot and then left before the white prospectors came. It was yet another one of those mysteries that nobody would be able to answer.

They continued to increase their gold production daily, and both felt that the next shovelfull would reveal a rich and productive vein. The evidence was overwhelming. They were eager and optimistic. Especially Red; he was as happy as he could remember being in a long time. He looked forward to his routine with Ray and enjoyed the company of Linda. It was a good partnership. They had filed the claim with Esmeralda County a week earlier, and they planned on filing with the regional office of the BLM in Tonopah the following week. It was all coming together. The final step would be the survey, and then they would be officially protected and on solid ground. In the meantime, they continued with their work.

~

Memorial Day in the old ghost town of Gold Point was unlike any small-town holiday event Matt had ever witnessed. Four solid days of celebrating the patriotic theme brought folks from all over to the desolate smudge on the map. The town swelled from the seven hearty souls who lived there permanently to about two thousand tourists, rock hounds, bikers, patriots, and their offspring. And they came from everywhere: Nevada, Pennsylvania, California, Arizona, Wisconsin, England, and Germany. It was an eclectic mix. Matt and Alex had their two daughters and their husbands with them, along with all four of the grandchildren. They were all staying at the cabin, including Thomas. Of course, he was the expert on the whole Gold Point experience now that he was almost ten years old and had a rich background in the surrounding events. "Now listen Jaybird, when they shoot off the cannon over there, it's going to make a very loud bang. Watch me and I'll tell you when it's time to cover your ears like this." He placed his hands over both ears and displayed the technique to his four-year-old cousin. Jayden dutifully followed his older and wiser cousin's counsel and mimicked Thomas' actions.

There were two performing stages set up outside the saloon for a bluegrass band and another country group. On Saturday they held the chili cook-off and on Sunday it was the Dutch oven stew contest. Matt thought Charlie should be there for that one. Then there was the brothel bed races where local ladies would dress up in the period dress of the late nineteenth century as soiled doves, and their men would race them around a course in a bed with wheels. They had pie and hot-dog eating contests and the winner of the chili cook-off won a Henry 44 magnum Big Boy rifle. The giant flag ceremony on Sunday was as touching and genuine of a tribute to our fallen servicemen and women as anything you would see at the Arlington National Cemetery. The flag was huge, probably forty by twenty-five feet. All of the attending veterans were asked to participate in the unraveling of the giant symbol, while one of the female country singers gave a heartfelt rendition of the National Anthem. Several of the old-timers kissed Old Glory as she was being unrolled. It was the genuine thing and Matt was right in there with them.

The most exciting event for the two grandsons, and Matt as well, was the frequent shootouts by the fake gunslingers walking around town looking for trouble. All in all, it was red-neck heaven and that included people of many shades of color, too. For everyone here, this event was an expression of the unity and love for their county. Race, ethnicity, and gender were not part of this celebration. The only thing that counted was respect for the country, and its servicemen and women. It was a step back in time.

As Matt walked through the dusty street holding the hands

of his two granddaughters Jenna and Erica, weaving their way through the crowd toward the ice cream stand, he saw it clearly this time. NOLES. The black SUV was heading north out of town heading toward the unpaved Willey road with a disrespectful dust plume following them. There were two people silhouetted in the front seat, but the personalized license plate was unmistakable. It couldn't be a coincidence. But that guy was from New York and it was at least fifteen or sixteen years ago when they worked him, and it was in Florida. That scumbag's plate was a New York personalized plate, not the Nevada one he saw, but it was too much for him to ignore. He wouldn't let it go this time.

~

Raymond and Linda got into the act and placed second in the brothel bed races. Red told him if he had given up the Pall Malls he would have come in first place. The winded Ray ignored him and downed another Budweiser.

That weekend at Pigeon Spring was one that Matt and Alex had dreamed about having for many years. Surrounded by their children and grandchildren, along with their daughters' husbands, all laughing and swimming in the pond, sitting by the campfire at night, and telling all sort of stories. It was the best that this life had to offer. It was why they had the ranch, and it was their reward for a life-long commitment to family life.

His son-in-law, Jeff, had Matt tell the ghost story of the haunted mansion, and while he was telling the story, Jeff sneaked off and then ran back into the campfire at the appointed time with a hockey mask on, yelling like the crazed psycho from the haunted mansion. It was a bit too much for the little ones, but after they saw that it was Jeff, they all laughed and chased him until they got to the end of the firelight. Then they scurried back to the safety of the campfire, just in case they were somehow mistaken and it wasn't really Jeff. When they all got up in the morning, they would go for a hike after breakfast and burn off some of the weekend calories. It wouldn't always be this way, but this weekend it was. This was what it was all about.

The hawks ignored them, and tended to their parental duties.

~

"Kiel, this is my cousin Derrick. He's got brass balls, he's smart, and he can follow directions."

"What's up? What you got in mind?" Derrick abruptly tried to get to the point.

"Kiel, let me explain, Derrick just got out of the joint in Ely about two months ago after a five-year stint for some stupid shit. He doesn't have a lot of social skills yet, but he's a lot smarter now, and I think he's somebody we could use."

Kiel had dealt with a lot of cons in his career, and he knew that the right one working with you could be a valuable asset. The key was if you got the right one. The wrong one could fuck up a good thing, but you needed them sometimes. Fuck it, he thought. If things went to shit because of this asshole, he would give up the loser and move on, just like in the past. "How's it goin', Derrick? Your cousin here is a smart guy. That's why he brought you to me. Here's what I need from you."

Derrick and his meth-dealing partner decided that since everyone in the county was in Gold Point for the Memorial Day weekend, now would be a good time to do it. But just in case they had any problems, both had hunting rifles and the meth dealer had a nine-millimeter Sig Sauer tucked down into his waistband on the right side of his dirty blue jeans. The ATVs were loaded up with the items they needed and they were on their way. The meth dealer had some of his product with him, too. It would help pass the time, and because they lacked any on their own, it would give them the courage they needed. They would be dangerous.

CHAPTER 11: THE RECORDS

When he was handed the unpatented mining claim, he accepted it as he would normally do, except for one thing. He didn't provide Raymond with a receipt.

"Kiel, he just filed the claim. I know exactly where it is. How about if I misfile it, so it won't be found for a while, or maybe I should just get rid of it. What do you want me to do?"

"First of all make a copy of it for me, but make sure nobody sees you doing it. Then I want you to put it in with some other documents that won't be processed for at least a week or two and make it look like somebody else in the office fucked it up, not you, maybe in with some real estate transactions or whatever. You know better than I do. Just make sure that nobody discovers the fuckup for a couple of weeks. I'll meet you tonight up at the Mizpah about six-thirty. The co-conspirators hung up.

"I'll file it first thing tomorrow, and I'll make out a receipt." The corrupt county official and the con man parted company.

~

"These morons are gonna freak out when they see us. We could just say they attacked us and we killed them in self-defense. They probably don't have any weapons, but we could fuck ourselves up a little with some shovels and shit. Make it look like they were beating us, and the only thing we could do was shoot 'em. And there wouldn't be any witnesses." Derrick liked the idea. It was an option, even though that smart-assed Kiel said he didn't want anybody getting hurt:. Typical of assholes like him. Have the guys with the real balls do the dirty work while he sits up in his big office and counts the money. The mother-fucker. They would do what they had to do.

They spent the rest of the day pulling out the R&R boundary markers and putting in ones of their own. They would use the ones they pulled out for the tonight's campfire so there wouldn't be any evidence. After setting up camp, they both did a couple of "lines" and enjoyed their high. They talked about how they would fuck these mother-fuckers up if they gave them any shit at all. They started to make themselves real brave for the upcoming confrontation.

His cousin at the courthouse had already filed the new unpatented claim in Derrick's name that Friday morning, and technically, if anybody checked, it was now his. Once all the dust settled, Derrick would make a phony sale to Macsvog International, and they would collect their money from Kiel. It was a piece of cake.

~

Raymond talked Red into staying with him and Linda that night in Gold Point. It was about a twenty-five mile drive by way of the old stagecoach road past Pigeon Spring to his camper, and he'd had a few beers, so he accepted their offer of hospitality. He didn't feel real comfortable staying at somebody else's place, but it was probably the right thing to do. The ghost town was pretty noisy though, especially for a ghost town. He wondered if he would be able to sleep with all of the racket. He wasn't used to it.

CHAPTER 12: THE FAVOR

"Hey Marty, it's Matt. Yeah, I'm up here in God's country living your dream." Because it was so expensive, he only used the satellite phone when it was absolutely necessary. Mostly it was reserved for emergency situations. They hadn't had any yet, but he never knew. There wasn't any cellular service in the immediate area, but if he traveled ten miles east on 266, he could get a strong enough signal. That was about a half an hour's drive round trip, and he wanted to get an answer to his question. "I was wondering if I could get a plate run and a criminal history on the name that it comes back to."

Marty was one of his local police contacts as well as a good friend. They came across each other a few years ago when Matt was working undercover for the FBI in the organized crime caper with "Fat Tony." Marty was one of the Metro police officers assigned to the elite local organized crime intelligence unit. They had been independently investigating the activities of Fat Tony and his associates — a number of high profile organized crime figures — including Sonny Blake. Metro received information from their informant that Blake came to Las Vegas from the Detroit area a few years before. He was previously a large-scale coke dealer with a lot of Florida connections. Then he had gotten out of the cocaine business, taken his substantial earnings, and bought into a local used car business. He also invested heavily in the booming Las Vegas real estate market with several straw partners. When Matt finally introduced himself to Marty at the FBI briefing as

"Sonny Blake," just before the massive roundup of the wise guys, Marty was pissed off big-time that the Feds had caused him and his unit to waste countless hours and resources on Sonny Blake. But he had to give the Feds credit; they never figured out that Matt was on their side until the caper unfolded, and since then, they became fast friends.

About fifteen minutes later, he called back. "Nevada personalized plate NOLES comes back to Kiel B. Sandefur, 423 Bridger Avenue, Tonopah, Nevada. It should appear on a 2008 Cadillac Escalade. No wants. No warrants. Except for a speeding ticket issued by the Nevada Highway Patrol two months ago in Esmeralda County, he's clean and even that was dismissed. What you got going on up there, a big organized crime horse theft ring?"

They laughed, and Matt said, "You know me, just following my nose. If there's anything to it, I'll let you know. Thanks for your help."

"Sure thing, Sonny." They both laughed again at the inside joke and hung up.

He needed to make another satellite phone call. "Hello, Mrs. Miester. Is Mr. Miester in?"

Gloria snickered and said, "Just a minute, Matt."

"Hey, what's up? I was just out in the garage polishing up the new golf cart."

"I'm just trying to make sense of something. Remember about fifteen years ago, when we worked on that Bureau special down in Miami?"

"Yeah, the big fraud case; the one where they had the offshore accounts in the Cayman Islands."

"Yeah, that's the one. What was that scumbag accountant's name? The one who lived in Ft. Lauderdale in the big mansion."

"You've been drinking, haven't you? Or the altitude? Matt, we're retired, remember? Do you need medical help?"

"Charlie, listen. Wasn't that guy's name Lionel something or other?"

"Yeah. I think it was. Yeah, it was Lionel Blanchard."

"Yeah. That's it. Wasn't the plate on his Mazzerati NOLES?"

"Yep, it sure was. I remember we followed him around so much; we got sick of seeing it. I think it was a personalized plate out of New York."

"That's it! That's what I thought!"

"Matt, forgive me, but I think you're a lunatic. What's this all about?"

After he explained, Charlie agreed with Matt. It was too much to ignore. Blanchard was a Florida State graduate and an obsessed Seminoles fan. Hence the license plate, NOLES. It could be a coincidence, but he had to admit, it was intriguing. It was a long time ago and in a different part of the country. NOLES could stand for something else too. Maybe it was somebody's name or nickname. It could be anything, but it was intriguing.

"Where are you going? The kids are getting ready to go on a hike."

"Alex, don't get mad. You know how I am when I get obsessed with something. I have to get an answer. Charlie is going to meet me at the Santa Fe in Goldfield in two hours. I'm sorry, and I know I told you those days are gone, but I have to go."

How many times had she heard that? She was angry, and for good reason, too. "You said that was it! Those days were over. It looks like it'll never be over. What's the point? You're going to go anyway. Just be careful, and take your gun. Tell Charlie I said hi." She gave him a hug and a kiss and let him go. She knew he would only be gone for a day or so, but those old feelings of loneliness came flooding back.

~

"Sergeant Marty Torgler, this is Lt. Davis from Internal Affairs. I need to speak with you down at IA, asap. "What's the problem?"

"I'll speak to you personally when you get down here."

"What the hell did those pricks want now? They probably heard that he badged his way into another UNLV basketball game or some other stupid shit allegation."

CHAPTER 13: THE SURVEILLANCE

It's just like old times. One last road trip. Charlie was glad to get out of the house and back doing what he did best.

"Charlie, I'm not sure I would remember what he looked like if it is him. It was a long time ago."

"Sure you do. Remember he had a weak chin and kind of looked like a rat with a ponytail." Charlie hated ponytails on men.

"Yeah, you're right. Didn't we nickname him "the rat?""

"That's the one, though I think you're off on some kind of wild goose chase. Didn't you say the plate came back to some other guy with a clean slate?"

"Yeah, but I have to find out for sure."

"What the hell, I wasn't doing anything anyway. I might as well hang out in the thriving metropolis of Tonopah." Charlie clearly needed more to do.

"When we get to Tonopah, let's ditch your truck at a gas station and find his address. I've got a printout from MapQuest, so we've got the directions. Once we have the layout, we'll do spot checks in separate vehicles until we get a visual. Maybe we can set up at a choke point where there are other vehicles and we won't draw too much attention. We probably shouldn't park in the neighborhood. It's too tight. If we get lucky, we'll get a look at him when he gets into his car. If not, we can intercept him at the choke point and play it loose until he stops and gets out. I've got my camera, so if you miss him, I'll be able to show you and we can either confirm it's him or not. We should have cell phone coverage in Tonopah, so I guess we can communicate with them. I'm not happy about not having better communications, but I guess it's the best we can do." It was good to see Charlie being the team leader again. The team went to work.

~

They got up late that morning; Linda already had the coffee ready and buckwheat cakes on the griddle. Ray had a slight hangover from his rendition of the brothel bed races and why he came in second. It had taken four more Budweisers to accurately describe every turn and twist of the event. Old Red didn't get to sleep until late because of the unfamiliar surroundings and the noise of the celebrants in town. They were getting a late start, and wouldn't get over to the claim until the afternoon.

~

"Give me another toot. I feel like I'm starting to crash. I want to be up for it when these fuckheads show up." Derrick did another line of methamphetamine. Because of their use of the extreme stimulant, neither one of them had slept since the day before and they were getting agitated and aggressive.

~

"Sergeant Torgler from the Organized Crime Intelligence squad is here to see you, Lieutenant." "Thank you, Colleen. Tell him I'll be with him in a few minutes." The Deputy United States Marshal continued with his briefing of the lieutenant in charge of Metro Internal Affairs "See Lieutenant, whenever an inquiry is made through the NCIC system it is red-flagged, and we are notified if it hits on one of our people in witness security.

We are notified automatically about who is making the inquiry. What we don't know is why they are checking him out. A lot of times, depending on the circumstances, we won't do anything, but just monitor the system for further inquiries. Maybe a local officer is simply writing a speeding ticket or the vehicle is illegally parked. It makes sense that he would run the plate. In this case, we know the protected witness is located several hundred miles away from Las Vegas and as far as we know, he doesn't have any Las Vegas connections. You know, especially in your line of work, it's not uncommon for the people who want to do our witnesses harm to ask a corrupt officer to do their bidding. I'm not accusing the Sergeant of being dirty, but you understand that we need to get to the bottom of it."

The U.S. Marshal's Service handled the administration of the federal government's Federal Witness Protection Program. Once a highly placed co-conspirator agreed to cooperate with government prosecutors and the DEA, FBI, or another federal law enforcement agency, and the agency was pretty much finished with them, and if a threat assessment determined that there was a real possibility of retaliation against the witness because of their cooperation with the government, the U.S. Marshal's service would take the witness. Sometimes as part of the plea agreement, the witness had to do time in a special federal prison with other government snitches, and sometimes they were simply given a new identity. Sometimes both things happened. It really depended on the deal they all agreed to.

Lt. Davis offered, "Well if you think there might be a problem with Sergeant Torgler, do you want Internal Affairs to work a case on him?"

"Has he ever been the subject of any suspicious activity in the past? If he hasn't, then I would say no." "Well, when I got the call from you, I pulled his personnel file. He has been involved in three shootings in eighteen years. All of them were deemed to be good shootings. He's received all kinds of "ataboys" from every agency from the Clark County Prosecutor's Office to the FBI and numerous departmental citations. He was reprimanded once for improperly displaying his credentials to gain entry to a UNLV basketball game. The Deputy U.S. Marshal said, "Bring Sergeant Torgler in."

~

When Matt and Charlie drove by the house, they were both surprised to see such a nice place in Tonopah. The home was a newer California mission style, complete with a faux bell tower and crushed red granite desert landscaping, accented with a number of Spanish daggers, a specimen blue palo verde as a focal point, and a beautiful kokopelli metal sculpture near the front entrance. Obviously it was the residence of one of the more successful residents of the former gold and silver mining Mecca. Matt was beginning to feel foolish for getting Charlie all stirred up.

"It looks like a pretty nice place."

"Don't forget he had a nice place in Florida, too." Charlie reprimanded Matt.

"I don't see anything in the driveway. It doesn't look like he's home. And the neighborhood looks a little tight, too. I think if we set up somewhere out near the main road near the intersection with U.S. 95, we might get lucky and pick him up turning into his street. There's a lot of through traffic with tourists checking out the shops on the main street. We could probably blend in around there. I'll take the first eye."

"I'll go on over to the grocery store parking lot and set up in there. Call me when you want me to take over the eye." The "team" went to work.

"Charlie, there's a "possible" that just went by my bow, heading northbound. Heading your way. I'll follow him loosely until he signals the westbound and turns towards you. I've got three for cover. I didn't get the plate. It could be a lookalike."

"Copy that. I'm waiting for him."

"He's gone on by the turn off to Bridger Street, still heading northbound. I'll stay with him for a little while longer."

"Copy."

"He's signaling a turn eastbound, near the Mizpah Hotel. I've got a light, but I can still maintain an eye."

"I'm moving your way. Have you been able to confirm the plate yet?"

"Negative, I still can't see it. The vehicle made the eastbound, and is parking in the lot on the north side of the Mizpah. I'm not in position to see him."

"Go ahead and break off, and I'll do a drive-by and grab the plate. Where do you think he might be going?"

"There's a pharmacy next to the Mizpah and an antique shop next to it. My guess is he went into the Mizpah."

"It looks like Nevada NOLES. No one is in the car. Let's meet at the grocery store parking lot. Charlie, what do you think?"

"Let's set up on the car, and I'll try to get a photo when he comes back. Why don't you check out the antique shop and the drug store? If he's not in either one of them, he's probably in the Mizpah. We'll concentrate on it if he's not in one of the shops."

"I told you, I don't know if I would recognize him after all of these years, but I'll give it a shot."

"Believe me, you'll recognize the rat if you see him."

"Nothing in the drug store or the antique shop. He must be in the Mizpah."

"Let's wait and see what happens with his car. It's still early, and I've got plenty of camera light. Matt, why don't you set up to go southbound if he comes out and heads that way? I'll be able to take him north if he goes in that direction. Let's play it real loose. If we lose him, we know where he lives, so we can always pick him up later. If it's him, as I remember, he's real "tail" conscious."

~

"Sergeant Torgler, this is Deputy U.S. Marshal Castro. He's got a few questions he'd like to ask you."

"I'm glad to meet you, deputy. What's up? Somebody rob the Wells Fargo stagecoach?" Marty thought the smartass routine would throw the Marshal off his prepared canned attempt to intimidate him. Anyway, he knew he didn't do anything wrong, so what ever it was, it was a fishing expedition on his part. As far as his highness the Lieutenant was concerned, he had too many years on the job to be worried about desk jockeys like him. He would stop just short of being insubordinate.

"Listen, Sergeant! You will NOT be disrespectful to this law enforcement official in my office! Do you understand?" Marty noticed his neck veins were sticking out, and the deputy was practically grinding his teeth. Perfect. Just the effect he wanted.

"No disrespect here Lieutenant, just trying to figure out why I'm here. How can I help you?"

~

As the groggy prospectors made their way over the mountain pass from Gold Point in the open-top Willeys, and down the winding dirt road toward Pigeon Spring, they decided to stop at the ranch and pay their respects before they headed out to the claim.

"Hey, Alex. Did the kids have a good time at Gold Point yesterday?"

"They sure did. Especially watching you and Linda almost take first prize in the bed races. It was so close. What happened?"

"I'll tell you what happened, Alex," Red belted out. "It's those damn Pall Malls. That's what happened." Raymond took a deep drag off his cigarette and blew a smoke ring in Red's direction. They were real partners now. "Where's Matt? Off on a morning ride?"

"He's off checking something out with Charlie. He'll be back sometime tonight or tomorrow. I hope he gets back before the kids leave for Las Vegas."

"It must be something important if he left in the middle of a family outing. Hope everything is okay."

"It's fine. He just had to go figure something out with Charlie. I think it's some old business of some sort."

~

"I'm gettin' real fuckin' aggravated with all this Davey Crockett shit. I'm about ready to tell your cousin to go fuck himself. As far as I'm concerned, he's costing me a lot of revenue. If these assholes aren't here pretty soon, my skinny white ass is out of here."

"Relax, they'll be comin' pretty soon. You got plenty of product. Have some more shit." The two new "mining claimants" were growing extremely impatient, and were ready for a confrontation.

~

"He must be in the Mizpah. You're Mr. Undercover; why don't you go in and check it out?"

"There's nothing I'd like better, but I'm starting to get to know a lot of people around here. Somebody might recognize me. I think Mr. Miester should make an appearance instead."

As Charlie walked into the historic hotel lobby, he headed toward the main dining room area and took a quick non-productive survey of the occupants.

"May I help you?" The hostess asked.

"No; I'm just looking for my girlfriend. I might be a little early. Where's the bar?"

"To your left, and around the flower arrangement."

"Thank you."

It was unmistakable. There he was. It was the rat. He was an older and fatter rat, and now he was almost completely bald, but he still had enough hair to pull together on the backside of his head to manage a small and disgusting ponytail. He was sitting by himself, pumping money into one of the dollar slot machines at the bar. The bartender was looming over him, and watching his every bet. Vocally encouraging his "wise decisions" on which cards to discard and which ones to hold. It was all part his tip strategy.

Even though Charlie had followed his every move for about three weeks when they worked him in Miami years ago, the rat never did get a good look at him. He could pull this off without a problem. "Good afternoon. What are you going to have today?" He started to order a margarita, but stopped short. He was spoiled when it came to margaritas. He would only be disappointed. Charlie was looking for a segue.

"What's he drinking?" He motioned toward the rat.

"He's drinking a Cuba Libre. It's a rum and coke with ..."

"... a twist of lime." Charlie interrupted the bartender and finished his sentence for him. "When I lived in Florida, that's all I drank. That sounds good."

With that, the rat lifted his predatory pointed nose up and away from the dollar video poker machine and pointed it toward Charlie. "I used to live in Florida. Where'd you live?"

All Charlie could think of was his rat-like appearance, and he replied, "Boca Raton."

The rat was now smiling at him. "I know it well. I used to live in Ft. Lauderdale. What brings you to this part of the country?"

Just then, Charlie's cell phone rang. It was Matt. "Is he in there?"

"Yeah honey, I'm just grabbing a quick refreshment. You go ahead and do a little browsing in the antique stores, and call me when you're ready to leave. I love you, too."

Matt knew that Charlie had made contact and he was with the rat. His hunch was right after all! What was all that Kiel Sandefur business about? He was probably hiding out from someone. One thing was for sure; he was up to no good.

~

As the Willeys made its way past the Palmetto ruins, the two partners talked about how they would follow the gold-laced quartz vein down into the earth and what they would do if it continued to head in that direction. "We might have to do some blastin' once we get into the harder stuff. I guess it all depends on what we run into." It was exciting for both of them just to talk about it.

"Listen, I think I hear somebody. It sounds like a car or ATV."

"Yeah, I hear it, too. Derrick, since you're on parole, and are not supposed to have a gun, take the rifle and hide behind that big rock up there. We don't know who it is yet. If it's them, draw a bead on 'em. When the time is right, I say we shoot 'em. You'll know when to do it, 'cause I'll pull out my nine and start blastin'. I know they said they didn't want nobody hurt, but fuck 'em. They're not here. We are."

"What the hell's going on? There's somebody else up here at the claim!" Raymond stood up in the moving Jeep.

CHAPTER 14: THE INVESTIGATION

"Matt. What the hell are you into? Some arrogant U.S. Marshal and a Lieutenant in IA with a broomstick up his ass just questioned me about the license plate and criminal history I ran for you. It seems he's a "special friend" of the government. "Let me guess; he's in the program, right?"

"He never quite admitted that much, but that's what it amounts to. He never would answer the question for certain. I'm sure it's against some bureaucratic bullshit regulation."

"What did you tell them about why you ran the plate?"

"What could I tell them? I told them I was working him, and he was involved in a case that I was putting together. Tell me I didn't just lie to a federal agent and the head of Internal Affairs."

"Lie is a strong word. I would characterize it as protecting your source of information."

"Look, Matt. What I just did was a fireable offense. Any remote chance that you might be able to save my ass and prevent me from losing my job, filing bankruptcy, and going through an ugly divorce from a pissed off wife? Not to mention my kids having to drop out of college, because their father, the former police sergeant, is now working as a greeter at Wal-Mart, and can't afford the tuition."

~

"I'm pleased to meet you Mr. Sandefur. My name is Charlie Miester. My wife and I left Florida about three years ago and moved to Las Vegas. We had a lot of investment property on the east coast of Florida and a shopping center we developed on the west coast near Naples in Bonita Springs." Charlie thought he would make the rat salivate at the prospect of getting into his fictional fat bank account. "We were made an offer we couldn't refuse. It was a lot of money, so we sold out and relocated. We were tired of the mosquitoes anyway. We vacationed in Las Vegas a couple of times a year, so we thought, what the hell, why shouldn't we just move there? I'm glad we did, too. We both play bingo every day, and we love living in Sun City. How about yourself?"

Kiel smelled cash. "A very similar situation for me, too: I was involved in several major real estate developments. Mostly resort condominiums and golf courses. We sold when things were really booming and I just thought I would like Nevada, the new land of opportunity. It's been great, too. This is still the place for the smart investor."

Charlie nodded. "Well just because I'm retired doesn't mean I'm retired from making money. I'm like you. I'm always looking for an opportunity."

The bartender interrupted. "If you're looking for business opportunities, Mr. Sandefur here has been the savior of Nye County. He's got the Midas touch. I've seen people I personally know double and even triple their investments with his company. The rat secretly grinned at the bartender's blind and misplaced endorsement. Another dumbshit was about to take the bait.

"Mr. Miester, here's my card. Please give me a call. Who knows? Maybe we can do some business."

~

"Have you heard anything from your cousin?"

"Not yet. They don't have any cell phone coverage out in that area, and even if everything goes right, I wouldn't expect to hear from them for at least a day or more."

"I hope they can handle it. I think Derrick is okay, but I worry about that meth freak buddy of his."

"Don't worry about them. I told you they're reliable. Besides, nobody can connect us to them. Sure, he's my cousin, but that's it. Everybody has a couple of black sheep in their family. It ends there. Besides, right now, he's got a legal right to that claim, so we can sit back and let the law do our work for us."

"Just make sure that he does what he's supposed to do. This might turn out to be a bigger deal than anyone thought. I've got a good feeling about this claim."

The rat hung up.

"Dawn, will you add a Charlie Miester to the list, please?"

~

When they got back to the Santa Fe in Goldfield, Charlie asked the bartender if he could make his own margarita. The bartender knew Matt and based on a head nod from him, the bartender let Charlie get behind the bar to work his margarita magic. He made an extra one for the bartender, and he tipped him for it, too.

"Charlie, you did great! I didn't know you had the undercover stuff in you like that. I'm proud of you!"

"Actually, I kind of got into it once I saw him sitting there, acting like he owned the town. I just did what you usually did. I just threw out a couple of things that I knew he wouldn't be able to resist, and bingo, he took the bait."

"That's exactly how it's done. "And you know what the

beauty of it is? He's supposed to be the expert at this kind of manipulation. You beat the best of the cons at his own game. He believes he's got a fish on the line. Your timing is impeccable, though. I just got off the phone with Marty. It looks like Uncle Sam is protecting our subject because of his unselfish devotion to the country. Marty is taking a lot of heat, because he is being a stand-up guy about the reason he was checking out this douche bag. He told them he was working a case on him in order to protect us. We need to somehow work up a viable case on him for Marty and get the venue changed to Las Vegas, where he has jurisdiction."

"Why don't we do something easier, like find the cure for cancer, or just dig up Jimmy Hoffa's body? Matt! We're not even law enforcement officers anymore. Remember?"

"Yeah I do remember. I remember something else, too. Under the law we would be called cooperating witnesses, and cooperating witnesses are not legally held to the same standard as law enforcement officers. Entrapment, fourth and fifth amendment issues, the Carroll Doctrine, and alleged agent misconduct, are all issues that law enforcement officers have to worry about, not cooperating witnesses. Once we bring law enforcement into the loop, then those standards come into play because we are working at their direction. Of course we would be held to higher moral standard than the normal cooperating witness, because of our background, if it ever went to a jury, but legally, we actually have more leeway than real law enforcement at this point. It's weird, isn't it? Private citizens can do more at this stage of an investigation than a trained law enforcement professional. Something's wrong with that. Let me see his card. Macsvog International. What the hell does that stand for?"

"Maybe it's somebody's initials or it's some acronym for something. There's something vaguely familiar about it though. We need to do a goggle search on it. Knowing him, he didn't just make it up. There's probably some hidden meaning to it."

"Are you heading back to Vegas, or are you planning on coming over to the ranch? Either way is fine with me."

They headed back to Pigeon Spring.

CHAPTER 15: THE CONFRONTATION

"Red. Stop the Jeep! I don't like the looks of this. Let's not make any mistakes here. Let's see what we're dealing with before we go on in there."

"I told you we shouldn't of put them boundary markers up. Look at that! By God whoever they are, the bastards took out our markers, and put some of their own in! The sons-a-bitches! They're claim jumpers is what they are!"

Derrick had a bead with the .306 on Red's forehead. He figured if he shot the passenger first, the driver would take off and he might get away. This way, he would be able to get another shot off at the passenger after he took out the driver. He was waiting for them both to get out. That would be the best. It would fit their self-defense story better. If they both did get out, he would shoot the younger one first and do away with him. Then he would get the old tall one. If he didn't get them, his buddy would for sure.

"Red. Stay here. I'm gonna look around. Keep the Jeep running."

Derrick deviated from his plan and shifted the rifle sites on the younger one. His heart was pounding and the rush was incredible.

As Raymond cautiously eased his way over the rocks toward the worksite, he saw the two ATVs and the smoldering campfire nearby. He yelled out, "Hey. Who's here? Show yourself." The skinny drugged-up partner started to walk out from behind a large volcanic outcropping with his pistol tucked down in his waistband. He was sweating profusely. Raymond saw the movement and froze in his tracks.

~

"Look who I found hanging around Goldfield," Matt called out to Alex. She looked like she had cooled off about him leaving earlier.

She smiled at her husband's friend. "Hi Charlie. You going to be staying with us for a while?" Alex was always happy to see her husband's former partner, plus he liked to do the cooking. That alone made him more than welcome.

"I'll probably stay the night if it's alright with you guys."

"Of course it's alright. Don't be silly. And you know you're welcome to stay in the cabin with us. You don't always have to sleep in that old camper, you know."

"Hey, don't be putting down my crib. It fits me like a glove." Charlie didn't like changes.

"I guess the kids left while I was gone," Matt commented.

"When we got back from our hike, they packed up and headed home. They told me to tell you goodbye and they said the same thing as I did. They thought that you had retired from the Bureau." She was still a little miffed.

"Did you find out what you needed to find out?"

"Alex you won't believe it. I've seen a personalized Nevada license plate on a vehicle around here a couple of times in the last few months. As it turns out, it's a guy that Charlie and I worked down in Miami fifteen years ago. I think he's running some sort of a scam out of Tonopah."

"What are you going to do about it? Are you going to let the Sheriff know or turn it over to the Bureau?"

"Neither. Tell her Charlie."

"Hey, you started all of this. You tell her."

"Somebody better tell me, because I'm starting to think that I'm not going to like what I'm going to hear." Matt decided to lay it all out.

~

As the tip of his index finger lightly stroked the sensitive trigger, beads of sweat were forming on his brow. He had a clear shot at Raymond, but he shifted back to the old, tall driver sitting in the running Jeep. He was surprised at his uncharacteristic composure. His partner would have to take care of the one on foot, because the driver would take off for sure once the shooting started. Old Red saw the brief flash of sunlight off the metal from the barrel of the rifle when Derrick switched targets, and yelled out to Ray. "Ray! I think there's someone up in those big boulders." Simultaneously, they heard the unmistakable sound of another vehicle approaching, just as the meth dealer stepped out. Derrick withdrew from his target and waited. Who else was coming? It was getting more complicated. Red yelled out again. "Ray. It looks like Linda." Derrick and his partner changed their plans.

"What the fuck do you want?" He walked threateningly toward Ray with his Sigsaurer plainly visible in his waistband.

"What do I want? I want to know what the hell you're doin' on our claim, and why you took out our boundary markers."

"Hey Derrick, you want to tell these assholes anything about *your* claim?"

With that, Derrick stepped out from behind the boulder with his rifle and said, "I believe you dipshits have it all wrong. I think if you check the records, this is my claim."

Red yelled out. "Ray, turn around and leave. We'll

straighten this out with the law."

"If you know what's good for you, you should listen to the old man, shithead, and get out of here while you still can walk."

Linda saw that there was something going on and instinctively stopped short. She got ready to defend them any way she could, and she grabbed a shovel from the back of her pickup. Ray called out to her.

"Linda! Get back into the truck and head back!"

"Good advice shithead. I wouldn't want to see your bitch get hurt."

Raymond had never acquired the taste for backing down, but he had acquired some smarts from his earlier encounters with irrational drugged-up psychopaths. This was not a battle he could win right now. He backed away and got into Red's Jeep. "Let's get out of here. We'll get some help." They turned around and left their claim.

"That looks like Red's Jeep heading our way, and I think Linda's right behind them," Alex called out. "Something must be wrong. I hope nobody's hurt."

The trio of Alex, Matt, and Charlie met them at the ranch entrance.

Matt yelled out as soon as they got within earshot. "What's wrong? It looks like there's a problem. Is anyone hurt?"

Old Red blurted out. "Not yet, but I'm thinkin' real serious about hurtin' some rotten claim jumpers for sure. The bastards are tryin' to steal our claim. They said they filed on the claim on our spot we been workin' for months."

Linda added. "They had guns, too. I think they would have started shooting if I hadn't surprised them like I did."

"Hold on. Hold on. Slow down. Let's start with who, what, where, and when. Ray, tell me what happened."

"Matt, you won't believe it," and he told him about the confrontation.

"The first thing we're going to do is contact the Sheriff." Matt retrieved the satellite phone and called for Esmeralda County Sheriff Ken Wilson. He and Ken had hit it off right away several years ago when they first met because of their common-law enforcement background. In fact, Ken had sought out Matt's help in getting assistance from the Las Vegas FBI office in a chop-shop investigation that was operating out of Dyer. Vehicles were being stolen in the Las Vegas area and transported and disassembled at a Dyer junkyard. As it turned out, they ended up busting eighteen people, sixteen of whom were from the Las Vegas area and were gang affiliated. Ken used it as a springboard to get re-elected the following year.

~

"Did you see those chicken-shit fuckers run? Man, I almost popped 'em!" Derrick was still filled with the drug-induced excitement.

"Yeah, if that scrawny little bitch didn't show up when she did, I was goin' to finish 'em off."

"This is the luckiest day of their sorry-assed lives, and they don't even know it. Let's get out of this shithole, and call your cousin. We can at least get a down payment on what they owe us." They did another line of meth and packed up.

"Kiel, I just talked to Derrick. They scared them off without any problem."

"Just wait until the dumbshits find out that they don't have the claim and it's Derrick's. That's when it's going to be fun to watch," Kiel snickered. They agreed to meet with Derrick and his partner on the north end of Tonopah at the Claim Jumper restaurant. The location seemed to fit the occasion. Kiel wondered if anyone would get it.

~

When Sheriff Ken Wilson arrived at the ranch, Matt and the group went out to meet him at the gate entrance. Ken only had ten deputies and four part-timers. Esmeralda County was over three thousand five hundred square miles, so he had to personally respond to many of the calls that came into his office. He wasn't just an administrator like his counterparts in other jurisdictions. His job was more like the sheriff of the old west. He actually did a lot of the lawman work himself. He looked the part, too: tall and lean with a bushy salt-and-pepper drooping moustache and a tan Stetson hat. He carried a not-so-western German made Heckler & Koch .40 caliber semi-automatic side arm, and instead of a horse, he drove a Ford Explorer 4x4. Other than that, he was the real deal.

Red, Raymond, and Linda told him their story.

"I'm going to go on up there and check it out."

"Ken, would it be alright if Charlie and I went up there with you? We know the way, and we'll stay in the background." Ken was appreciative of the respectful manner that Matt used. He realized that Matt and Charlie had extensive training and experience in these matters, but they didn't try to remind him of it. He would welcome their help.

"Of course you guys can. I would appreciate the company," and they headed out in Ken's 4x4. Both were authorized by federal law to carry concealed weapons, so Ken was happy for the rare backup.

"It looks like they cleared out for the time being. It's like they were here just to make a show with Red and Raymond, and once that happened; their job was done. Let's look around."

Charlie called out that he had found something. "Hey, check this out. It looks like a used plastic baggie. It probably had some kind of dope in it. There's a small amount of residue left."

"I've got some presumptive test kits in my car. Let's see what we've got." Ken went to his police vehicle. "Yep, it looks like it's meth. It tested positive. Unless Red and Ray are into speed, I would say whoever these guys are, they're meth freaks. Our friends are very lucky they didn't get hurt. These guys are dangerous. I think I'll be a regular fixture around here for a while. These "citizens" need a little oversight I believe."

When they got back to the ranch, Red, Raymond, and Linda were waiting for them.

"First thing tomorrow morning, I'm going over to the county courthouse and check on the claim. We'll see what's going on."

"That's a good idea, Ray. After you do, stop in my office and let me know what you found out. I need to know a little more about our "friends" here. In the meantime you guys shouldn't go up there until I'm able to get this resolved. With these guys carrying guns around and using meth, someone's gonna get hurt, and I don't want it to be you two." Matt and Charlie agreed with the sheriff.

~

"You guys look like shit. You want anything to eat?" Kiel asked. "No thanks, we ate just before we left, but I could use a cold coke," Derrick lied. The methamphetamine seriously suppressed their appetites. They couldn't eat even if they wanted to. "Me, too." His partner grunted.

Derrick's cousin asked in a hushed tone, "So how'd they take it?"

Derrick and his partner both started laughing, and he told them. "You should have seen the look on those assholes' faces when they saw us standing up there on *their* claim. At first they looked pissed off beyond belief. Then when they saw our guns and the new boundary markers we put in, they knew they didn't want any piece of us. They took off like a couple of pussies. You won't have any problems with those two dipshits."

Kiel said, "I know you don't want to hear it, but it's real important for us to pull this off the right way. You guys go back up there and stay a few nights a week for a couple of weeks until this all dies down."

"That's bullshit! Do you have any idea of how far out in the boondocks that place is? I'm not getting paid enough to sleep out there like I'm some kind of a fuckin' jackrabbit or something!" Derrick's partner protested. Maybe he could get a few more bucks out of these two pricks by doing so. "You haven't even given us anything for what we've done already." That should do it. The tight bastard.

"Will you relax? We're not finished here yet. I'm going to take care of you," Kiel hissed through clenched teeth. "Let's finish talking. Then you'll get paid."

Good; his protest worked. When he clenched his teeth, Derrick's partner thought Kiel looked like some kind of a rat or mole.

"In a couple of weeks Derrick will sell the claim to Macsvog and you'll get the balance of what I owe you." They continued to discuss the details of the scam.

Just before the meeting broke up, he handed them both a thousand dollars in separate envelopes. "See, I came prepared to take care of you guys. We're all business associates in this matter, and we're all going to make some money." The meeting broke up.

Just like he thought; nobody got the Claim Jumper restaurant joke. The dumbshits.

CHAPTER 16: THE RECORDS

"What do you mean you don't have any record of me filing the claim?" Ray didn't want to take out his frustration on the young female clerk, but he was upset. After all, she was only doing her job. "I was in here not too long ago and filed the claim. I paid the filing fee in cash and did everything I was supposed to do."

"Do you have a receipt for the transaction?"

"What receipt? I didn't get any receipt."

"That's quite impossible sir. We always provide a receipt." He could see he wasn't getting anywhere. "I'm sorry ma'am. Could I speak to a supervisor? I'm very confused about this whole thing."

"Certainly. I'll get one for you." She brought out an older woman and introduced her as her supervisor. Ray repeated his story.

"I'm sorry sir, I checked on the plot numbers that you provided, and a claim has recently been filed by another individual. The file shows that he paid the required fee and as far as this office is concerned, he is the rightful claimant at this point."

"Can you give me his name?"

"I'm sorry, I can't at this point, but it will be posted on our county website soon. You will be able to view it as soon as it is posted."

Ray went directly to the Sheriff's Office and met with Ken Wilson. "Sheriff, I don't understand it. I went into the Recorders

Office, filed the paperwork, and paid the fee. I even remember what the guy looked like who I paid it to. He described the official.

"I think I know who you're talking about, Ray. I'll ask him about it. Maybe there's some paper mix up or something. I'll try to get it straightened out. In the meantime, remember what I said. I don't want you guys going up there. Let me follow up on this."

~

"Hi, Sheriff. What brings you over into the dusty old Recorders Office?"

"Hi Sandy. Is your boss in?"

"He's out to lunch. Do you want me to have him call you when he gets back in?"

"Please do."

~

"Kiel. The Sheriff was over here at my office asking for me. What should I do?" The county official was beginning to panic.

"First of all, quit shaking in your shoes. He's going to know there's something wrong as soon as he talks to you. Get yourself together and give him a call back. Answer his questions and deny any knowledge if he asks you if you know anything. He's just fishing around. He doesn't know anything. As long as you remain cool, it won't be a problem. Just relax. Call me back when you get done with him."

"Hey Sheriff. Sandy said you wanted me to call you. Is there anything I can help you with?"

"Thanks for getting back to me." He told him about Ray's situation. "That's real strange Sheriff. Sandy told me about that fellow coming in here and said he had filed on the claim first, but we don't have any record of it, and I don't have any recall of it myself … and he thinks he talked to me, huh. I can't remember anybody like that, but if anybody in this office did accept the claim and the fee, we would have given him a receipt, and filed it. Sandy says that he didn't have any. Do you think he is lying, Sheriff?" This was going easier than he thought. "Hold on Sheriff. I'll get the name for you." He gave him Derrick's name. He would find out eventually anyway. Kiel was right. It was a piece of cake. What a smart man. "If you need anything else from me Sheriff, please just give me a call."

He called Kiel right away. "You were right, Kiel. He was just fishing. Besides, nobody can prove anything. I just denied ever processing the claim and that was it. When Derrick shows him his receipt, that should end it. He's got nothing."

~

It was a good thing that the weather was accommodating Derrick and his partner. Otherwise they would have abandoned their new claim in spite of what that asshole Kiel had wanted them to do. It was a good thing, too, that they had an ample supply of "product." It would be unbearable if they didn't. They passed the time by target practicing on some empty beer cans. Derrick thought that his marksmanship was improving. He wondered if it was a positive by-product of the meth use. Even though it made him jumpy, for whatever reason, he was able to get a clearer site picture than usual. He seemed to be able to react quicker, too. He practiced his draw from the hip. He was definitely faster on speed. He laughed. "That's why they called it speed." He said to himself.

"Hey! I thought you brought more water than this. We're almost out, you dipshit! Now what are we gonna do?"

Derrick's partner responded, "Well, I guess you're going to Dyer to pick more up! Dipshit! That's what you're gonna do! After all, I'm supplying the crank. The least you can do is go get some water. If they want us to stay up here, then you'll have to get us some. Take my truck." Derrick needed a break from him anyway. He headed out toward Dyer in the old sun bleached light blue Chevy Silverado half-ton pick-up.

~

Charlie and Matt drove out to the Timbisha cemetery just outside of Lida. Matt photographed the recording device in Charlie's hands with the grave marker in the background. It was a good thing he had learned how to get a good depth-of-field with a camera at the FBI Academy years ago. With the date stamp on the film, and the clearly focused inscription on the gravestone in the background, there would be no doubt that when they taped the call, they were on the Indian reservation.

Under Nevada Revised Statute 200.620 & 48.077, it was unlawful to intercept a telephone conversation unless one party to the communication consents, *and an emergency situation exists, making it impractical to get a court order permitting the interception.* It was the second part of the statute that might make the tape recording unlawful, and therefore inadmissible. The Nevada law did have a loophole however; Nevada statutorily allowed the admission in its courts of the contents of any communication lawfully intercepted under the laws of another jurisdiction, *if the interception occurred in the other jurisdiction.* The Federal statute of one-party consent without the requirement of a court order applied on a government reservation, such as the Native American cemetery where they now stood. It seemed like a lot of trouble to go through, but both Matt and Charlie had seen too many great cases dismissed on stupid technicalities just like this. Besides, they had good cell phone coverage in Lida.

~

"Macsvog International. How may I help you? Hello Mr. Miester. Let me see if he is in." She checked the list. He was on it! "Mr. Sandefur, I have a Mr. Miester on the phone. He wants to speak with you. He's the new one that I just added to the list," she said.

"Put him through, Dawn. Thank you."

"Hello, Charlie. How's it going? I didn't expect to hear from you so soon. What's going on?"

"Sorry to bother you, Kiel. I know you're a busy man, but I was talking to a few of the guys on my senior softball league here in Sun City in Vegas about some of the rates of return that your company has been seeing, and well, I think there's a lot of interest down here. Most of these guys have quite a bit of money, and like me, they are always looking for ways to make a little more. They asked me if you would be willing to come down here to Las Vegas and make a presentation. Honestly, I think it would be a great deal for all of us. What do you think?" *The greedy fucks never learned.*

"Sure we could set something up. Like I said, the board of directors are probably going to be limiting our options in the near future, but if we move quickly, they may be able to take advantage of the situation. I say we set something up."

"That's great! Give me a couple of days, and I'll get it organized, and get back to you." Charlie said.

"I look forward to getting together with you and your friends soon."

It never failed. The more money these assholes had, the greedier the dumb fucks got. Sure he would meet with them. *And he would take their money too.* The greedy fucks!

It was time to call. He would be relieved to see the case come his way. Matt made the call.

CHAPTER 17: TURN IN THE ROAD

He shifted the old pickup out of four-wheel drive as soon as he passed through the Palmetto ruins, and headed out onto State Route 266. He made the westbound turn toward the California state line and started toward Dyer. Even though Dyer was in Nevada, Derrick had to pass through a small swath of California before the road headed north again and back into Nevada. It was only about a five-mile stretch. The speed limit was sixty-five, but he could easily do eighty-five in this remote area.

The California Highway Patrol aircraft clocked the vehicle at ninety-two miles per hour and radioed the description of the vehicle to the counterpart sitting at the entrance to the Oasis Ranch in his CHP patrol car, under one of the twenty or so giant cottonwood trees that lined the roadside. "Copy that shadow unit. I've got him heading toward me. Stand by." The patrolman lit him up about a mile-and-a-half before he would have re-entered the state of Nevada. The patrolman immediately called in the 10-28 on the vehicle plates to his dispatch, knowing already that the registered owner had several run-ins with the law in Nevada even before he approached the pickup. He unlatched his holster and had his right hand on the pistol grips as he cautiously walked up to the passenger side of the truck. CHP had revised its policy several years earlier that required them to approach the driver's side and now permitted the passenger side approach. As he got closer to the vehicle, he spotted the .306 with the scope lying on the floor of the back seat with several spent cartridges spread out on the seat. He drew his weapon and ordered Derrick out. He proned out him next to the pavement.

Sheriff Ken Wilson lived in Dyer and altered the daily seventy-five mile one way trip to Goldfield either by going north to U.S. Route 6 and on into Tonopah and then south on U.S. 95 into Goldfield, or by taking Nevada State Route 266. The distance was about the same either way. Today he was heading home on State Route 266.

As he approached the arrest scene, he recognized the young CHP officer as Steve Stallworth. Steve's father Richard had been a police officer in Yuma, Arizona, and took a round in his shoulder during a drug raid with the DEA task force he was assigned to. He took a disability retirement and moved to Dyer when Steve was thirteen years old. Ken had known him since he was a kid, following his promising career as a star high school quarterback in Tonopah a few years back and later on at UNLV. His football career ended with a brutal sack by the linebacker buddy of a competing quarterback during a practice session his second year, which blew out the anterior cruciate ligament of his left knee. It was a deliberate hit. His athletic endeavors over, he concentrated on getting his criminal justice degree. He did it in just three years. Steve had served briefly as an Esmeralda County deputy sheriff under Ken before he became a CHP patrolman.

The Sheriff hit his lights and pulled up behind the CHP officer. "Looks like you could use some company Steve. What you got here?"

"Sheriff, I'm glad to see you. I'm not sure what I've got. I could use your help, though."

"Let's start by getting him cuffed and searched."

"Well, it looks like we might have a small amount of controlled substance here," the trooper said, and pulled out a baggie of meth from Derrick's left front pants pocket.

"Derrick! I've been wanting to have a little chat with you anyway. How fortunate we should meet under these circumstances. My name is Sheriff Ken Wilson. I think we should have a little talk. Steve, would you mind?"

"Not at all Sheriff. I love chatting. Especially with our friends who are felons, on parole, in possession of a firearm, and are found to be holding a bit of controlled substance on their person. I think it will be a productive chat."

~

"Where the fuck have you been? I thought you said fuck it, and stole my truck. Why you been gone so long?"

"First of all, I'm pissed off. You didn't have a spare tire, and I had a flat. There was a guy that stopped to help me and he had some Fix-a-Flat. That got me into Dyer. Then I couldn't find anybody to fix it or sell me a tire. I even went up to the north end of Fish Lake Valley to that junkyard for some help, and they're out of business. Finally, I stopped at the hardware store, and they called some mechanic named Bill to plug the tire. Here's your fuckin' water, asshole." He bought the cover story.

~

Even though the giant bullfrog was less than three feet away from him, Matt didn't notice the big amphibian sitting next to the partially submerged log mixed in the with the watercress until the animal moved and gave up his position. The rough texture of the log was mimicked by the texture of his skin, and the color of the pond vegetation perfectly matched the subtle hues of greens and the darker colors in his skin pigment. Even his body shape furthered the illusion, with only his dark eyes peeking out above the still water. It was amazing to Matt that the forces of nature and evolution all worked together in such harmony to produce the effect. Countless generations of the species must have endured an astronomical number of chromosomal minute changes, and a lot of trial and error to get to this point. Nature was just like everything else. It depended on practice, experience, and luck to get good at it.

~

"Matt, can I talk with you and Charlie in private?" Sheriff Wilson asked. "I think I know what's going on with Ray's and Red's claim." He told them about his encounter with Derrick and what his new informant told him about his uncle and Kiel Sandefur.

"You guys have had a lot of experience with these kind of things. How do you think I should investigate this? What would you do?" Charlie and Matt looked at each other and grinned. "What? Did I say something funny? You guys aren't turning into a couple of federal assholes, are you?"

"No. No. Ken." Matt said. "It's just like there is some kind of divine guidance going on here." He told the sheriff about Sandefur, Macsvog International, Florida, the witness protection program, and their plan.

CHAPTER 18: THE NEWCOMERS

That night, just before she drifted off, she thought about the lives of those who came to this place before she did. The remoteness. The loneliness. The hardships. Nancy Walker. Alex slept.

~

The long walks seemed to somehow temporarily suspend the anguish and loneliness that sometimes overwhelmed her. She probably should just leave and go on back to where she came from. Both of her parents had passed since she left the rolling green pastures of Carroll County, Ohio more than five years earlier, but her two sisters still lived there with their families. She could go back with them and help raise her nephews and nieces. She could help out on the farm, too. She closed her eyes and had a difficult time picturing their faces for a moment. She remembered them as they were, but that was a long time ago. The children would have changed much since then. She pushed these thoughts and others like them in her mind together like a dam holding back water. It helped to keep the other thoughts out. She could only do it for a while, then the dam would break, and the unwanted thoughts would flood through. Then she would have to live it all over again.

It had been four months since her beloved Joseph was caught in the cave-in, and the life was crushed out of him and three others. It took four days of crews working round the clock clearing the rock and debris before his mangled sad body could be recovered. All three were buried at the small cemetery in

Sylvania.

Nancy remembered the exact moment when she first spotted him at the Carrolton Feed Lot down on Amsterdam Street. She was with her father and his hired hand, the old negro Chester, loading grain and supplies. She was just twelve years old, and he was fifteen. At first she thought that he was much older, because he was tall for his age. Joseph's uncle, James Walker, owned the feed store, and agreed to put his brother's son to work after the family fell on hard times following Joseph's father's death from infection. They lived over in Jefferson County in New Somerset. They locked eyes on each other and then mutually smiled. Despite seeing one another other on at least eight more occasions, they didn't speak for another six months.

As these thoughts were flooding in and out, she walked and looked at the ground near the giant white boulder, trying to build up the dam again with other thoughts so she wouldn't have to think about it for a little while again. That's when she saw it. She picked it up. It was immediately added to the dam of thoughts. She could use it to help block out the painful memories for a short while. The arrowhead was beautiful! Who put it here? She would make a necklace out of it with the new twine-like ribbon she had been keeping since last Christmas.

They got married when she was sixteen, and eight months later Joseph got the offer to go out west. He had learned the farrier trade over the last several years from Jessie, the local blacksmith next door to the feed store, and had acquired some experience with mules, too. The Irishman, Mr. Dunnihoo, had been talking to him and several others about heading out to the new goldfields in western Nevada. "Even if you don't prospect, there's plenty of work out there for a good farrier. You can do a little prospectin' on the side, too. Hell, anybody can strike it rich. Maybe even you. I've got a deal for you. If you shaw my animals free for two years, I'll pay the way for you and the Mrs. to go to Goldfield, Nevada. That's where we're goin', and that's where we're gonna git' rich. You two can stay with me and Mrs. Dunnihoo until you get a place of your own." Even the young weren't exempt from the lure of the gold county. Joseph and Nancy eagerly accepted. They left two weeks later.

The first part of the trip was an adventure full of newness and wonder — the greatness of the mighty Mississippi river, the vastness of the prairies, and the soaring peaks of the Colorado Rockies — but nothing prepared them for the harshness of the brutal Mojave Desert. The bleak openness of the terrain and the relentless unforgiving heat of the scorching sun was beyond anything they had ever experienced in the gentleness of the rolling green slopes of eastern Ohio. After a while, they learned how to manage and adapt, and they soon realized that even though it was vastly different from anything in their young experience, the desert had an understated beauty that existed no where else on earth. The openness and starkness and even its meanness was to be appreciated. It was unforgiving, hard, and delicate ... complex. Light played a greater role here than in their homeland, and distance was a lie. It captured them, and they embraced their new adopted state, Nevada.

As different as Ohio was from the Mojave Desert, so was Goldfield from Carrollton. Whereas their hometown was quiet, slow paced, and a place where life centered on the family and farm, Goldfield was loud, raucous, and life centered on liquor, whores, and gold.

After three weeks in Goldfield, Mr. Dunihoo heard about the prospects in the Pigeon Spring and the Palmetto Wash areas, as well as the new findings around Sylvania.

"Joseph, we're heading out for the Pigeon Spring area. It's about sixty-five miles west of here, and they got a little camp goin' on out there at the stamp mill. They got a store and roadhouse, and a couple of other things goin' up. It's close to Palmetto, and it's only about six miles from another mining camp called Sylvania. I hear they're bringin' in a lot of rich ore to the stamp mill for processing. They need a good horse and mule-shoer, too. What do you think?"

"When do we leave?" Joseph asked. They headed out two days later.

On the way, they stopped at the town of Lida to rest the horses and themselves. They only had ten more miles to go, but the horses had to navigate the 7,400' Lida summit before they started the descent on the other side down toward Pigeon Spring. Lida was a smaller version of Goldfield, with all of the same "amenities," but on a much reduced scale.

Joseph and Nancy wandered over to the blacksmith shop, while the others freshened themselves up. The horseshoer was bent over holding the left rear foot of a line-backed dun gelding and taking a rasp to the hoof.

"Hi there, mister, how's it goin?"

The grisly old farrier didn't even look up. He answered him with a gruff, "What'll you need?

"Nothin' sir. I just was curious about the business, that's all."

"Curious about my business? I'll tell you what. I could use three good horseshoers, and ain't none around that's not diggin' for gold. That's how business is. Everybody wants everything done yesterday! I can't do it all. Hope you're not expectin' me to do anything today."

"No. No, I was just askin.' That's all." Pigeon Spring would be a good place for a horseshoer to make a living.

Two days after their arrival at Pigeon Spring, Joseph had set up a makeshift farrier shop. It consisted of little more than a hitching post and a nearby pinion pine for shade. The first day he did all four shoes on three horses and one sixteen-hand mule. The folks around the tiny mining camp and the surrounding area were glad to have an experienced farrier in their midst. Nancy got a job in the small roadhouse serving meals to passers-by, and hungry miners who got tired of cold beans and rainwater and needed a change of diet. She enjoyed talking with them and hearing about the families they left behind in places like Wolf Run, Missouri, Bergholz, Nebraska, and Springfield, Tennessee. They equally enjoyed her company because they were reminded in a real way of the wives who were waiting for them back home, and the familiar softness of a gentle woman, not like the whores that they sometimes visited. She liked the roadhouse owners Mr. and Mrs. Scott. They reminded her a lot of her own parents. It was a good match for them, too, because they had lost their daughter, Emily, who would have been about Nancy's age, three years earlier from snakebite. Nancy looked a lot like her, especially from the back.

The Dunihoos continued to be helpful to them while they were getting settled, and even gave them a miner's tent Mr. Dunnihoo had won in a poker game from a drunk prospector. It needed some attention, but with a little thread, and a couple of hours of needlework, Nancy was able to make it waterproof again. They set it up not far from the farrier shop, and after lining the dirt floor area with some large flat rocks that they found on a hillside south of the spring, they made it their first home. It would do just fine until they could build something more substantial.

They continued to improve upon their lives for several months. Even though business was good for him, Joseph heard every day about the ones that struck it rich, and his thoughts began to turn toward finding some gold of his own for their future. "It doesn't make any sense. Here we are in the middle of the biggest gold rush this country has ever seen, and I'm shoeing horses. I'm young and strong. I should be out there with them. I can always shoe horses later on."

"What about those people who are counting on you to do farrier work?" Nancy asked.

"I can do that when I'm not prospecting. Besides, what did they do before we got here?" Nancy had to admit that he had a point. She didn't want to be the one to hold him back, so she encouraged him to join the others. First he had to learn the business, so he signed on with the deep shaft hard rock outfit over in Sylvania. Nancy stayed on in Pigeon Spring.

At first, Joseph rode back to Pigeon Spring every night on horseback and left every morning long before sunup. Nancy could see how the daily trip was taking its toll, and encouraged him to stay in Sylvania at least three nights a week. He reluctantly agreed to it, and even though they missed each other's company, it was a lot easier on him that way. On Sundays they made sure that they spent all day with each other, and oftentimes went exploring and prospecting on horseback. Joseph had spent a lot of time with the old experienced prospectors while passing the nights in Sylvania and was beginning to learn about what to look for in the landscape for a promising 'show.'

After a couple of years, they had accumulated enough money to build a respectable one-room house. Joseph purchased lumber from the lumberyard in Goldfield and brought it in on two wagonloads. He and several friends from the Sylvania mine helped him and they had it up in a week-and-a-half. Joseph had managed to dig out a part of the hillside on the east side of the house and made a root cellar. Nancy could store ice in it, too, and it was cold well into July. The house was only about fifty yards from the spring, so getting water wasn't a huge ordeal.

"Let's go north this Sunday. We haven't been out that way for a long time. I've been wanting to take a better look at things out in that part of the country." Joseph said.

They headed out after an early breakfast and took the wash north of Pigeon Spring. They followed it for several miles until it narrowed into a canyon. They climbed out before the canyon walls got more vertical and headed west. They were in thick pinion pine now, and continued their ascent. As they stopped to let the horses rest and nibble on the sparse grass, they could look down on Pigeon Spring far to the south. Folks were getting ready for the day, the morning fires of the settlement sending small plumes of smoke into the fresh mountain air. The big timbers of the stamp mill looked almost insignificant from their high perch. They continued west and then north again. As they made their way toward a steep narrow canyon, Joseph began to recognize the type of volcanic quartz-laced outcroppings that the old prospectors told him about.

"Nancy. Let's tie up and look around a little bit." They found a nearby pinion and after loosening their mounts' cinches, went off on foot. Joseph was intrigued by the appearance of what looked like a small "stope," or the beginnings of an excavation at the outcrop. It looked like someone may have started working the area and given up years ago. He could still see the overburden of consolidated materials lying about, but weeds were poking up through it, testifying to the passing of time. He took his small farrier hammer out of his saddlebag and began chipping at the outcrop. He saw what he was looking for. Gold!

"Nancy! Come over here and look! You won't believe what I found! It's gold!" They both jumped into the air and hugged and danced and yelled. Joseph chipped off a large part of the debris and exposed the precious yellow metal to the light of day. He broke off a piece about the size of a thimble and held it up to the sunlight for inspection. They couldn't believe their good fortune. They spent the rest of the day chipping away at the outcropping and planning their future.

It was decided that he should keep working at Sylvania until the end of the month when he would get paid, and use the money to stake their new claim. In the meantime, they would do their best to cover their tracks and keep their find a secret.

Their future together ended when they finally brought his mangled and bloodied body out of the dark unnatural gaping hole in the side of the mountain.

Despite the outpouring of support from the fledgling community, and the help of Mr. and Mrs. Dunnihoo, the Scotts, and others, Nancy's world as she knew it was forever changed. The love of her life was taken away. He was gone. Forever gone. She was lost, and she was pregnant. She had missed her last period and was waiting to see what happened the next month before she got him all excited and made the official announcement.

From the moment she picked up the spearhead, the overwhelming dark pain in her heart began to diminish for the first time in several months. It was if she was being healed from within. The unbearable loneliness and despair became balanced with her other thoughts. The pain did not dominate her mind. It had a place of its own. It was still there, but not before everything else. She could let the dam go, and the unwanted thoughts would not come flooding in like before.

The following Sunday, she saddled up her horse and headed out early. She took some of her husband's tools with her. She was pleased to see that nobody else had stumbled across their claim. She spent the day chipping away at the outcropping, and was amazed at the size of the large nugget she uncovered.

~

Wallace was still drunk from the night before, and instead of walking it off, he eased his hangover by drinking some more whiskey. He was getting low on it, so he would have to make a trip into Pigeon Spring soon to get more. He needed some more beans and coffee, too.

She saw him at about the same time as he saw her. "Why, hello there sweetie. What's a pretty young thing like you doin' way out here all by yourself? Hell! You're that young new widow. Ain't ya?"

She didn't like the way the drunk was looking at her, but she tried not to show her fear.

"What you doin' there? You workin' a claim? Hell! You shouldn't be doin' that. You need a man to do that. You probably need a man to do other things, too!"

Her heart was beating and she couldn't contain her fear anymore as he stumbled up the slope toward her. "You stay away or I'll …."

"Or you'll do what? Scream? Go ahead. Ain't nobody around here gonna hear you." He grabbed her blouse and tore off several buttons. She screamed for help and hit him repeatedly with the hammer she held in her hand. It only seemed to enrage him more. He strangled the life from her body.

The gold nugget he found in her saddlebag was the biggest single nugget he had ever seen. When he was done with her, he loaded her lifeless body on the back of her horse and led it several miles south. Before he stuffed her body into a rock crevice, he took the spearpoint necklace from her still body and put it in his pocket. "She won't be needin' this anymore."

When her horse came on into Pigeon Spring without her the following day, the Dunnihoos organized a search party to find her. Just to make it look good, Wallace Stow joined them. When they found her, at first they thought that she had fallen into the crevice and died from the fall. Then they saw the evidence of the brutal rape. It was a sad day for everyone at Pigeon Spring when they buried her east of the stamp mill.

The night of the funeral, Wallace Stow got more intoxicated than he usually did, and he couldn't stand having the spearhead in his pocket anymore. Maybe if he got rid of it he could get rid of the guilt. He threw it as far as he could up on the ridge west of where he was camped. "Good. It was gone." Now maybe he could sleep. Without the whiskey, he couldn't ever again.

CHAPTER 19: THE SALES PITCH

As Kiel walked toward the meeting room at the senior's center at Sun City, they were just about to serve lunch to the twelve or so retirees who were assembled for his lunch presentation. Charlie greeted him at the entrance to the meeting room and thanked him for coming to speak to the senior softball league members. Among the retirees was Sergeant Marty Torgler, an IRS agent from the criminal investigative division, and the FBI supervisor from the Las Vegas white-collar crime squad. The remaining retirees were really retirees, but they were all were retired cops or agents. Marty, the IRS agent, and the FBI supervisor, were all wearing recording devices.

Kiel viewed the group much like a shark viewed chummed water. This was going to be sweet. By the time he got done with these greedy fucks, they'd be giving him their grandchildren, he chuckled to himself.

The Assistant United States Attorney said that the investigation would have to show at least one hundred thousand dollars in fraudulent losses before he would authorize prosecution, but in this case he would be inclined to prosecute on far less because of Sandefur's prior background and his misuse of the Federal Witness Protection Program. Once they executed search warrants and contacted his clients, the investigators were certain that they would surpass the U.S. Attorney's threshold amount. The case also would be enhanced by his outlandish claims of unreasonable returns as well. If they could get that on tape, it would help.

Charlie asked. "Kiel, what sort of rate of return can we expect?"

"That's really why we're all here now, isn't it Charlie?" Kiel said. "You all are experienced investors, and you know that the best prediction of future performance is past performance. With that having been said, many of our investors have enjoyed returns of 75 to over 250 percent within a year. It all really depends on the timing of the investment cycle. Right now, the cycle is expected to peak in the next two weeks. At least that's what our market analysts are saying."

He could tell that they were soaking it all up. He finished his presentation with phony charts and a lot of intimidating financial babble. He wouldn't be surprised if he hooked all of them with his impressive presentation. He concluded with handing out his business card and encouraging them all to contact him personally. He reminded them that they needed to act quickly if they were expecting to maximize their investment due to the upswing in the investment cycle. The greedy fucks.

~

"Now listen, Derrick, what the Sheriff needs from you is confirmation of your story about your cousin's role in stealing the claim and Kiel Sandefur's involvement on tape." Matt gave the new informant his instructions. "Remember, your freedom is at stake here. And I don't think you want to go back to the joint for another five years."

Sheriff Wilson looked at him and nodded. "That's right, Derrick. You better not mess this up. If you do, you're the one who will be the loser. Got it?"

"Don't worry about me, Sheriff. I know exactly what I have to do."

~

"Listen, cuz. I need to meet with you and Kiel. I want to know how long we're going to have to put up with this phony scam. I was under the impression that we would only have to do this for a few days. We're gettin' real tired of shittin' in the woods, if you know what I mean."

"Will you relax? It's not like what you two are doing is heavy lifting. All you two have to do is camp out and enjoy nature. Some people work all year long to have a camping vacation like you guys are having. Relax and enjoy it."

"Enjoy it! Have you ever tried camping out with a psycho? I'm getting real tired of his company. Do you know that he shot a nine-millimeter directly into a rock right next to me? It ricocheted off and just missed my head. He needs a diversion. Maybe we could get a couple of broads to go up there with us for a few days. What'd you think?"

"I don't know if that's such a good idea. The less other people know about what we're doing up there, the better. Hey! Where are you calling me from anyway? I thought you didn't have cell coverage up there."

"I had to get away from the psycho for a couple of hours, so I drove over past the Lida summit. At least I can make a few calls from here. Anyway, set something up with Kiel in Tonopah in the next couple of days. I want to talk about when we're going to finish this up, and how much we're going to get paid. The psycho is getting real edgy, so we need to get some answers soon."

"I'll get hold of him. Call me tomorrow about the same time, and I'll let you know where and when."

"Okay, cuz. Talk to you tomorrow."

~

"How was that, Sheriff? You convinced that I'm on your side yet? I don't think he suspects anything. Do you?"

"That was real convincing, Derrick, but that was the easy part. Let's see how you do when you actually meet with them."

Matt followed with, "That's when you'll have to control yourself so they don't see anything different in how you're acting. I've seen too many people in your shoes who do everything they're supposed to do, but give it away by the way they're acting. I've even seen them non-verbally give up the fact that they're wearing a wire by gesturing that fact and the crooks try to clean themselves up on tape. I'm happy to say that in every case that I found that to happen, the deal was off and we threw the book at the cooperating witness. Don't let that happen to you. You understand? Oh, and one more thing. It's not *our side* you're on. It's *your side* that you're on. You screw this up and it's back to the can for you. Understand?"

"Yeah. I understand. Now can we get out of this graveyard? It's freakin' me out."

After Derrick left, Matt and the Sheriff decided to call Charlie to see how the meeting between the new "investors" and Kiel went.

Then the Sheriff and Matt decided that they needed to meet with Marty, the FBI, and the IRS before they made their next move. This caper was beginning to look like it might be wise to form a task force with the other agencies. From what Matt could tell, he could see several possible federal violations involving Macsvog International, now that it was established that Sandefur was criminally involved with a public official. Hobbs Act, bribery, and fraud: they were all predicate acts for the powerful Federal RICO statute. Not to mention the fact that once they pulled telephone toll records and searched Macsvog records, they would probably discover victims of his scam all over the country. They would need the U.S. Attorney's clout to pry information out of the U.S. Marshal's Witness Protection Program administrators to figure out where else Kiel had operated and where there might be other victims. It was getting interesting.

"I think we need to set up a Group II undercover operation, and run it as a task force. We'll partner up with Metro, and the IRS. With the Group II special funding from FBI Headquarters, Charlie could be the designated undercover, and make an investment of $50,000 or whatever they will authorize, and we'll follow the money. In addition to that, we'll start to write a Title III affidavit seeking wiretap authority on Macsvog International's office phones and Sandefur's cell phone. We have enough probable cause right now to get us there, especially with the new informant that Sheriff Wilson recently developed."

The FBI White Collar Supervisor made a persuasive argument with the Assistant United States Attorney."We have a special obligation to vigorously pursue this matter. He's used the government and in effect has made us an unwitting partner in his criminal activity."

The Assistant United States Attorney replied, "Hey. You can stop there. You've convinced me that we need to work him, and I think the task force concept will work well here. I'll talk to my boss and let him know that we have agreed to prosecute, providing you guys make the case. I'll set aside some grand jury time next week and you can give an overview of where you plan on going on the case. Matt, can you and Charlie continue to assist the FBI case agent?"

"I can't speak for Charlie, but … wait a minute. Yes I can speak for Charlie. Count us in. I heard him say a hundred times how he'd be an FBI Agent for nothing; now's his chance. We're in."

They all laughed because they had heard the same line from him as well. "Good luck gentlemen. Let's meet again in two weeks for a status check."

After the meeting, Tony Riggio, the FBI White Collar Supervisor, asked Matt what his thoughts were on who he should assign as the case agent. Matt had to give him credit, because Tony knew that without the right case agent acting as the ramrod, even the best cases could be sidelined. Even cases where things fell into place encountered obstacles that needed to be skillfully maneuvered around. Issues with FBIHQ, the Department of Justice, the U.S. Marshal's Service, the Undercover Unit, the Informant Unit, the Legal Unit, and Accounting and Special Operations. And these were the ones that were supposed to be on the good guys side. All of the bureaucrats who couldn't investigate their way our of a paper bag would be trying to put his/her two cents into the pot just to justify their existence — all done from the impersonal remote distance of Washington, D.C.

The truth was, they were all a hindrance and viewed as such by the real agents who did the real work. Matt recalled all the times he had attended in-service training sessions on various matters at the academy at Quantico throughout the years. These FBIHQ managers would get up before the group and talk about how they managed this case or that case, all from the perch in this unit or that unit, not even realizing that for those experienced agents sitting in their audience, they were viewed as a joke. They were seen merely as obstacles. Of course, they viewed themselves as necessary oversight who were chosen to provide guidance and counsel for the dunderheaded, constitutionally challenged mere agents. The thing was that most of them who were chosen only had a couple of years of street experience before they eagerly raised their hands to get out of the field because they knew they couldn't professionally survive the gritty street work of the Bureau. They would be found out! That was the good thing about Tony. He was a street agent at heart and was a supervisor for all the right reasons. He'd been there.

"How about George Lyford? I know he's transferred to the Reno Resident Agency, but he's still in the division." George had been on the Public Corruption Squad with Charlie and Matt as a young first office agent. He was a former Marine and had been a street cop in Buffalo, New York. He had worked undercover on the B.P.D. Narcotics Squad prior to coming on board with the FBI and had a lot of experience dealing with difficult informants. Prior to being sent back to the Las Vegas Division, he had been transferred to the Miami Office, where he worked a major police corruption case as the case agent. The crooked cops were basically working for several major drug dealers providing protection. Of the fourteen indicted, two became cooperating witnesses, eleven plead out and received lengthy prison sentences, and one committed suicide. "If you can get him, he'll get the job done."

"Good choice. I'll see what I can do."

"Tony, tell him that if he turns us down, I still haven't forgotten the entertainment at his bachelor party. I think he'll come around. Also, we'll have to have the new informant meet with the subjects in the next couple of days. He placed a consensually recorded phone call to his cousin yesterday and requested a meeting to discuss things. I don't think we can put it off. Besides, it would be a great opportunity to run Charlie in on them during the meeting and pick up incriminating conversation through the informant on tape after he leaves."

"Great idea. I'll get the necessary authority, open the case, and notify Special Operations for surveillance."

"Don't forget to get Lyford down here. It's time for him to start working again."

"And Matt, by the way, we don't use *tape* anymore. It's all digital."

"Whatever. I just hope it works better than the crap we had to work with before I retired."

"It does." Tony respectfully smiled at the veteran retired agent.

~

"S-2 to S-8. The source is walking into the restaurant now. I have the eye."

"Copy that, S-2. We are monitoring him on channel three. Let's give him plenty of room."

"Copy that, S-8." The surveillance team was set up on the Claim Jumper restaurant watching and monitoring Derrick's meeting with his cousin and Kiel.

"Well, you don't look any worse for the wear. Besides needing a good scrubbing and a shave, you look like any other outdoorsman around here." Derrick's cousin tried to minimize his disheveled appearance.

"Blow me! I know what I look like, and it ain't pretty. What's going on with this thing anyway? Is there a problem that I should know about?

"What do you mean? We told you that we had to go slow and make it look like it was a legitimate deal, and it would take a little bit of time until we could make the sale to Macsvog," Kiel replied.

"Yeah, but you didn't say anything about it taking this long. We want our money and we want to get out of there."

"Listen, that dumbshit prospector went to the sheriff and complained that he had been fucked over and his claim was stolen, but he doesn't have a leg to stand on. You've got the receipt for the claim filing and the claim is filed in your name. He doesn't have a chance of getting it back. I say we give it another week and then we do the phony sale to Macsvog. Then you get your money and that's the end of it."

"Hey, Kiel. I thought that was your car out front. How's it going?" Charlie acted like the rat was his long-lost best friend.

"I'm doing great, Charlie. What are you doing up here? I didn't expect to see you again for a while."

"I'm looking at a piece of property over near Chadavich Creek for an investment. You know that big ranch selloff in ten-acre parcels."

"Yeah, I sure do. I think that thing is going to go big time in about another year. It's a good deal."

"I'm sorry. I didn't mean to interrupt. I just wanted to say hello. I also wanted to tell you that the guys are very interested in your proposal."

"That's great, Charlie. Tell them to give me a call, and I'll get them started. How about you?"

"With me it's a done deal. I'll be ready to go forward in a couple of weeks. Is it still going to be available?"

"I think so, but remember what I said about the investment cycle. I wouldn't let it go much beyond a couple of weeks. It just might be too late after that. Let me know what you want to do soon."

"You got it. I'll give you a call in a few days. See you."

"All right, Charlie. Take care and tell the guys hi."

"Gentlemen, that is what I call a dumbshit greedy fuck. It's guys like that who make my life worthwhile, and at the same time, make me a lot of money. These greedy fucks already have more money than they can spend in their lifetime, and they just keep wanting more. I'm going to relieve them of their cash and they won't even know it until it's too late. The greedy fucks!"

"What do you mean, Kiel? You mean you're gonna scam him?" Derrick said.

"Of course I am, you dipshit! You think I would do anything else with these greedy fucks? Stick with me and your cousin and you'll make more cash than you ever did jerking around with drugs."

"S-8. Did you copy that?"

"I did. Let him finish the meeting, and then back off. We don't want to spook him at this point."

"Copy that, S-8. We'll let him go after the meet."

The tactic of Charlie running into Kiel and his co-conspirators did the job. It would be difficult for Kiel to argue that he lacked the intent to defraud when it came right out of his own mouth. The U.S. Attorney would like that, and so far Derrick did what he needed to do in order to stay out of jail.

CHAPTER 20: A MOUNTAIN OUT OF A MOLEHILL

"I'll tell you, Matt. I'm having a hard time keeping old Red from goin' up there and kickin' someone's ass. I thought he would cool off a little bit once the Sheriff got involved, but he didn't."

"I know he's upset, but he's just got to understand that he has to back off, especially now. Charlie and I have worked up a game plan with the Sheriff and a few other folks for our friends, the claim jumpers, and if he does anything he could mess it all up. I really can't go into detail, but you guys have just got to trust us. He needs to just have some patience."

"We trust you Matt. I just think he's so upset, because this is the first time in his hard life that he has been this close to a real bonanza, and these bastards are trying to take it away from him. It's what he has dreamed about all his life and now when he can practically taste it, these thieves are trying their best to hoodwink him. I think he's afraid they just might be able to do it, and this is his last chance. He's not getting any younger."

"Tell him to sit tight and give us a couple of weeks. It'll all work out."

~

"I should have known you two old farts were somehow involved in this caper when Tony told me I was being temporarily assigned back to the Las Vegas field office as the case agent by request of somebody from the past." George Lyford tried to act like he was put out by the temporary reassignment, but he was flattered that the two old farts demanded and got him for the job as case agent. He had to admit when he looked around the bureau division, the experience level was a little on the thin side. When he was fully briefed on the case, he agreed that he was the one for the job.

"It sounds like you guys are well on the way. What's the status of the Group II request to FBIHQ for project funding and the Title III wiretap application?" When he saw his supervisor, Charlie, and Matt return a mute grin, he knew the answer to his question. "That's why I'm here, right?"

"George, you're not as dumb as everyone says you are." Matt replied, and they all laughed, even George.

"I guess I had better get started with the wire tap affidavit first."

Most people outside of law enforcement think it is a relatively simple matter to get a wiretap authorized by a federal judge, but it is a grueling process with ridiculous layers of oversight. It begins by writing the document, which basically tells the story of the investigation in minute detail. It includes all of the basic intelligence, history, and logical attempts to address the ongoing criminal activity with conventional and traditional techniques. There is a "need" section in which the affiant has to demonstrate why it is necessary to use such an invasive technique. There is a "minimization" section that identifies who can be listened to, and what types of conversation can be recorded. Unless the conversation involves identified subjects of the investigation, generally they can not be monitored. If the conversation is a privileged conversation with an attorney, or a member of the clergy, normally it can not be monitored. And if an agent violates these restrictions, he will be the subject of an internal investigation. In addition, every ten days the authorizing federal judge has to be provided a report of what happened the previous ten days. Even before the affidavit is submitted to the court for authorization, it has to be reviewed by the squad supervisor, then the Office Legal Counsel, the Special Agent in Charge, the U.S.Attorney, the Department of Justice in D.C., and several layers of FBIHQ officials. It is an absurd process. Most affidavits end up being a short book of about eighty pages or more. But it is a great investigative technique if you can get one authorized, and that is why most agents put up with the triathalon. George was a bulldog and he knew how to get it done. "I'll have it done in three days." Matt, Charlie, and Tony had no doubts that he would.

~

They had been on line for four days and had received incoming calls from all over the county from unsuspecting victims. One eighty-three-year old World War II disabled veteran who was trying to raise enough money to get a cornea transplant for his wife of sixty-three years was clearly scammed out of his life savings of $122,000. Kiel even bragged about it to Derrick's cousin in a related phone conversation. In another call Kiel made, he misrepresented himself and his company as major contributors to a children's cancer research center. They even monitored him placing calls to his contacts in the U.S. Marshal's Service and having them run license numbers for him under the pretense of somebody suspicious being in the area. He was out of control and using everyone he could.

Derrick's cousin was hanging himself, too. Besides the scam that they were involved in trying to steal R&R Mining, the task force intercepted fourteen other calls between the public official and Sandefur that were related to other attempts to gain inside information on claim filings and other sensitive documents filed with the county. Several were especially incriminating because the acts were committed with an attached "quid pro quo" demand from the county official.

"Kiel, I hate to say anything to you, but I'm taking a lot of risk here. I've got the Knapp mining file for you, but I'm going to have to get some money from you. Like I say, I hate to say that, but my ass in on the line."

Kiel responded. "Don't I always take care of you? Meet me tonight. I've got a grand for you. You don't think that I expect you to do this for nothing, do you?"

The FBI surveillance team covered the meeting later on that evening in Tonopah and got video of the payoff.

The task force also intercepted several calls between Kiel and a large-scale Florida-based cocaine dealer. While it didn't appear that he was directly involved in the transaction, the FBI and DEA were able to add the specifics of the conversations to the information the Florida authorities already had on the dealer. The result was that the Florida agents seized a hundred kilo cocaine shipment in the resort community of Naples, Florida without Kiel even knowing that his big mouth had helped the feds.

"Gentlemen, as you all know, we are coming up on the last week of the thirty-day authorization for the Title III. So far, it's been extremely successful. What are your thoughts?" The Assistant U.S. Attorney was pleased with the progress of the case. At the meeting were all the key task force members, including Sheriff Wilson, Matt, and Charlie.

The supervisor, Tony Riggio, added, "I've seen a lot of cases that were great and going along fine until the greedy factor came into play. The Bureau got everything it had hoped for and more in the first thirty days. Instead of ending it, the agents got greedy and extended it and then that's when the unexpected happened. The subject discovered the investigation, or an agent's car got burglarized and sensitive documents ended up in the wrong hands, or the informant went south on them. I say if everyone in this room agrees that we've met our original objectives, then let's end it. Charlie, Matt, Sheriff, what do you think?"

Matt added, "I agree, but before we do, I think we should tickle the wire a little. Create a situation and see if he takes the bait. Give the case a little more jury appeal."

The case agent George looked bewildered and added, "I think it's got a lot of jury appeal. We've got scams of elderly disabled World War II veterans and cancer victims being misrepresented, drugs, and public official corruption. We've got everything except murder. What else do you want?"

"I think you just said it: murder. And not just murder, but murder for hire." Matt and Charlie laid out their plan.

CHAPTER 21: A TANGLED WEB

The incoming call registered in at 3:55 p.m. and the monitoring agent recognized both voices immediately, as well as the caller's number. "Kiel, I need to talk with you and my cousin right away in person."

"Listen, I already told you, we are almost done with this thing. You'll get your money next week." Kiel was getting irritated with Derrick's incessant demands to finish the caper and get paid.

"No, no, that's not the problem. We've got something else going on. It's important! You're not going to like what I have to tell you."

"All right, but it better be important! Meet us at the restaurant at six tonight. I'll call your cousin."

"I don't know what that scumbag cousin of yours wants, but he says it's important to meet us tonight at the Claim Jumper. He sounds nervous. I hope he's not coming apart on us. Remember, you vouched for him."

"Kiel, I told you, he's solid. Don't worry about him. Did he say what the problem was?"

"I already told you I didn't know what he wants. At first I just thought it had something to do with his bitching about getting paid and getting out of there, but he said that wasn't it."

"Whatever it is, I'm sure it's not any big deal. See you tonight. Hey, maybe we can stop at the Bunny Tail later on."

"Maybe; we'll see."

~

"All right, we're here. What the fuck do you want?" Kiel was not in a good mood.

"Hey, don't get pissed at me; I'm just trying to keep us all from fucking this up, that's all."

"What's the problem?" Kiel relented.

"Well, I don't know just how to handle this, and I need some direction from you guys."

"Look, quit beating around the bush. What's going on?" Kiel was twitching his rodent-like nose.

"You know that douche bag partner of mine? Well, he's talking crazy. He's telling me that unless he gets a hundred thousand dollars from you, he's going to the Sheriff and tell him everything. In fact, he may be an informant anyways. He told me that he had to cooperate once a couple of years ago to get out of a drug charge."

Kiel practically hissed back through clenched teeth. "You said you could trust him. You motherfucker!"

Derrick's cousin looked around to see if anybody else in the restaurant heard Kiel's outburst. "Hey, I thought I could! I didn't know about any of this shit until just now! When he told me this, I came right to you." The blood was draining out of his face and he looked like he just might faint. "Kiel, what are we going to do? We're all going to jail! Maybe we should confess!"

"Will you shut the fuck up? You're acting like some little bitch! Nobody's going to jail!"

Derrick continued. "Kiel, I don't know, but I think he's serious. Plus he's all fucked up on meth. He's liable to do anything."

"Anything? Anything? Anything, like accidentally shoot and

kill himself?"

"What do you mean?" Derrick asked. Even he was shocked at where he thought Kiel was going with this.

"Look, he's a nobody dope dealer. You said so yourself more than once. As far as I'm concerned everyone would be a lot better off if something happened to him."

"What do you mean, "If something happened to him? You mean kill him?" Derrick's cousin looked like he was going to piss his pants right on the spot. His eyes were darting around the restaurant like one of those lizards you see on the Discovery Channel. "Kiel, we can't do that, it's murder!" The corrupt public official could barely vocalize the word.

"I didn't say 'us'; I mean Derrick. He's got the perfect alibi. The dumbshit is out at the claim high on speed and fucking around with his firearm and accidently pops himself in the head. Who's going to say otherwise? Derrick could even say that he came back from wherever and found him there dead. Otherwise, you're right. We're probably going to jail, and you'll really be somebody's bitch. Is that what you want?" He just looked back at Kiel with his mouth half open and didn't say a word. "I didn't think so. What do you think, Derrick?"

"Well I know I'm not going back to prison for any reason. If that's what it takes, that's what we have to do. When do you want me to do it?"

"Hey, the sooner the better. And although I shouldn't give you anything for it since you brought him into us, I'll give you ten grand after it's done. Just bring me a picture of him after you do it."

"I'll call you after the hit. Have my money ready." Derrick got up and left.

~

"S-2 to S-8, it looks like the source is about ready to rap up the meet. Do you want us to follow the subject?"

"Negative. Let him go. Let's stay with the source. Keep it loose." The SOG team followed Derrick for about forty-five minutes without his knowledge, just to see what he was up to. He made a series of tail-checking evasive moves that weren't a problem for the experienced surveillance team to handle, even in the small community of Tonopah. Afterwards, he headed south on U.S. 95 to the small town of Beatty about ninety miles away, and went directly to room 213 at the Motel 6, just as he was instructed to do by his contact agent for the debriefing.

Oakley Utter, the contact agent, was not easy to impress. The salty veteran was in his last year of his almost thirty-year-career as an FBI Agent, and he had seen and done it all. "Derrick. Where were you in the old days, when I was out developing cases and making my bones? I would have been the friggin' FBI Director if you would have been with me in my younger days. That was probably the best consensually recorded conversation I ever heard *one of our guys* have with a couple of scumbag plotters. You deserve an Oscar!"

In spite of the fact that he had turned on his own cousin to save his ass, he was proud that the experienced agent recognized his efforts. And he liked the sound of *one of our guys.* Derrick would be eager to please him the next time he betrayed his cousin and Kiel. The "Oak" knew how to work these sources. But Derrick was wondering how he would talk his speed-freak partner into posing for a dead shot.

~

Sheriff Wilson looked at the dead meth dealer along with Matt and just shook his head and grinned. The matted blood in his hair was attracting flies, and his eyes had that glazed-over look that the deceased have. "Can you put some more debris on the right side of his head just above the ear? That's it! Push it into his hair. Now move his left arm so it's folded in an unnatural twisted position along his left side. That's it! Now move back.

"Whatever you do, fuckin' do it fast, 'cause these flies are eating me alive," the "deceased" drug dealer mumbled out, the sound muffled by the dirt in front of his mouth.

"Just hang on for another minute, and we'll be done," The FBI photographer said as he was snapping the photos. "There. I think we've got just what we want. Here Matt, take a look."

The Sheriff and Matt peered into the camera's viewfinder. "Looks good to me," Matt said.

"Me, too," added the Sheriff.

"Can I get up now?" With that, Kurt James aka Jessie James, drug dealer, meth addict, and *informant* for Sheriff Ken Wilson, pulled himself up out of the dirt and took the wet paper towel that the photographer handed him. He tried his best to rid his face and hair of the chicken blood, dirt, and weeds that had drying and adhered to him.

James was one of those on-again-off-again informants who were sources for law enforcement only when they were jammed up or otherwise looking for a way out of whatever troubled situation they found themselves in the middle of. Usually they were reliable, because they knew if they lied or failed to produce, they were going to jail. It was a great motivator: jail.

Such was the case for James. When Sheriff Wilson and Matt first approached him at the claim when they knew Derrick would be elsewhere, he immediately rolled over on Derrick, Derrick's cousin, and Kiel. He even gave up his source of supply for the meth he was dealing. Now both Derrick and James were informants, but neither one knew about each other's secret life. It was a great way for the Sheriff and Matt to test the veracity of both.

CHAPTER 22: ALL THAT GLITTERS

Since Matt and Charlie were spending a lot of time in Esmeralda and Nye Counties recently on their case, Alex decided to take some time off from work and spend a couple of weeks up at Pigeon Spring along with the horses and her dogs. Matt and his sidekick Charlie usually showed up in the evenings and spent the night and part of their days there, so at least she had some company part of the time. She'd rather be at the ranch and be with Matt some of the time rather than stay in Las Vegas and not see him at all. He had taken a two-week vacation from the casino, and had assured her that the case was making a turn toward the finish line. She had heard that from him before, too.

She remembered when they were still in the Detroit FBI office and he volunteered for the undercover assignment in Cleveland. It was a police corruption case where the crooked cops were shaking down illegal gambling operations. The Bureau had decided that the best plan of attack would be to set up an illegal gambling operation themselves, manned by FBI undercover agents, and see what happened. Matt had extensive prior experience in working illegal casino type operations and said that he was just going to help get them started. And that really was his intention, she was sure of it. But soon he was running an illegal, but US Government sanctioned, craps game and casino on the west side of town. Through the help of a top notch informant and his Cleveland Bureau partner Ray Morrow, he was so intertwined in the operation that it turned from him just helping them get started to being one of the main characters in the project. It would be two-and-a-half years later before their lives became somewhat normal again. Forty-two bad cops plead guilty and went to prison.

But he was right about this one. This case came to *them*. Matt didn't go looking for it. There wasn't any volunteering on his part. In fact, *they* were about as far away from where anything should be happening that it was like this was supposed to happen: Like it was meant somehow to take place. She thought it interesting that she used the term *them*.

That night Matt, Charlie, and Alex discussed the case developments over dinner. Matt often found that when he would discuss a complex case with her, she would sometimes ask a simple question about an innocuous fact or event that was overlooked by him. On more than one occasion she had prevented a disastrous ending to an otherwise successful case. Like the time he had gotten court authorization to steal a drug dealer's car at a Detroit shopping mall and install a hidden microphone. Even though Matt had an undercover agent accompany the crook on a shopping spree at the mall, and he wouldn't come back for his vehicle until the undercover agent was notified that the installation had been made and the car returned, she asked: "What if he looks outside and sees that his car is missing? Maybe you should put a similar car in the spot until you're done with his."

Prophetically, the drug dealer did just that. It was a nice car, and he was worried about it being stolen. "Hey where you goin'?" the undercover agent asked.

"Hey man! I paid a lot of money for that motherfucker, and I ain't got no theft insurance on it. I want to make sure the "Chairman" is okay." He loved his recently-acquired Mercedes

AMG and even gave it a name. With that, he walked out to the entrance right in the middle of the installation and checked on the Chairman. The Chairman's "cousin" was sitting right there where it was supposed to be: Murphy and his law. Fortunately, Matt had listened to Alex. So he had learned over time to pay attention to her questions and observations.

"It sounds to me like Derrick's cousin doesn't want anything bad to happen to Jessie James or Kurt, or whatever his name is. From what you've told me, he doesn't want him killed. He just doesn't want to go to prison, and it sounds like he's just going along with the scheme because he's intimidated by Kiel. That's just my opinion, but I don't think he's on board with the whole thing. I'm not convinced."

Matt and Charlie realized that if she weren't convinced, then no way would a jury of twelve be inclined to say unanimously he was the bad guy that the government would be portraying him to be. They would probably lose the murder-for-hire case against the corrupt public official and maybe put the entire case in jeopardy. They had to figure out a way to shore up the contract murder case against Derrick's cousin or just drop the whole thing.

Later, Charlie headed back to his camper and Matt and Alex sat next to each other on the cabin porch swing looking west at the smudge of light left from the long-gone red-tainted sunset, now well behind the Sierra Nevada. The crescent moon was just starting to rise in the east, and as Alex got up and looked to the south, she could see the crown jewel of the night sky, Mars, starting to show itself low on the horizon. Before long the late summer sky would yield the constellations Ursa Major, Lyra, Aquila, and the Milky Way. They would appear so close and thick that she would feel as if she could reach out and touch them. She wondered who else stood in this very same spot looking at the same night sky, thinking the same thought as she did right this moment.

There was silence between them, each having their own thoughts. Neither felt obligated or compelled to interrupt the quiet of the night by talking. Their comfortable relationship allowed it to be so. After a time, Matt broke the stillness of the night. "I think I'll go check on the horses before I turn in."

"Why don't you take a few carrots down and give them a snack?" Alex replied, and said, "I think I'll get ready for bed, too."

~

It was not a familiar place, and she was sure she had not been there before, but she had no difficulty finding her way. It was as if she knew where she was going, but not quite déja vu. It was more like she was viewing an old familiar video with somebody else operating the video player. It was Nancy Walker, and Alex was watching her movements as she walked toward the old garage. She approached the building as if she had ownership of it. The foundation was made of the local stone boulders and located to the right of the main entrance was a faded painted white number 142 on an equally faded light blue background. The number was barely readable. The side door was open, so Nancy went in, and Alex followed her. There were several chickens inside the garage pecking at the ground, and none took notice of Nancy or even Alex as she followed her. The garage now looked more like a small workshop or an old small barn that had been converted to a garage sometime in the past. Nancy went through an open doorway that led to a back room full of miscellaneous junk, old electric motors, a few over-used tools, and several rotted cardboard boxes of more junk. Nancy went over to the back of the southeast corner of the room and stopped. She held her gaze for several minutes looking toward the area where the rock foundation met the building. Then she did the most remarkable thing. She slowly turned from the corner and focused her gaze directly into the eyes of Alex and pointed toward the corner. She gave Alex an almost imperceptible smile and nod. Although she wasn't sure why, Alex felt herself return the gesture.

~

"It's a risk, but I think it's a risk we should take." George Lyford gave the green light to have Derrick make contact with his cousin and record the conversation. "If the conversation goes the wrong way, there's nothing that says we have to charge him with the conspiracy in the hit-for-money plot. The illegal use of his position "under the color of official office" still stands alone under the Hobbs Act, although the recorded conversation would be discoverable by his defense."

They made the decision to have Derrick make a cold contact with his cousin, and not give him an opportunity to think about things by forewarning him with a phone call. Derrick had taken a real liking to his contact agent Oakley Utter and was motivated to do a good job. Even if was against his own cousin.

~

"What are you doing here? You shouldn't be seen with me around here!" Derrick's cousin whispered an admonishment over the clerk's counter, his eyes darting from side to side checking to see who was looking at them.

"I just came in to check on the registration of my claim with the county. You can't be too sure if these public servants are doing what they are getting paid for." Derrick smiled at his uptight cousin.

The county official offered in a low and irritated tone, "Meet me north of town at the turn-off toward Silver Peak in fifteen minutes." Before going back to block-stamping some form, he looked around again to see who might be watching them.

When he pulled up next to Derrick's car, he was sweating and looked worried. "Did you do it yet?"

"No. Not yet. I didn't know if you really wanted me to do it. You know I don't have to. In fact that's why I came to see you. Are you sure you want to go through with this?" Derrick asked.

"Am I sure? I don't see any other way. I mean if this asshole is going to turn us in, I say it's him or us. The sooner you kill him, the better I'll feel. If I had the balls, I'd do it myself. Just get it done, and get it done fast before he starts blabbing his mouth."

"Okay. I just wanted to be sure."

~

"Shadow one to S-8. It looks like the CW is finishing up with the meet." The high-flying surveillance SOG aircraft relayed to the surveillance team leader.

The Assistant United States Attorney listened to the recording, looked at Matt, Charlie, and George Lyford and smiled. "I guess on top of being a corrupt public official, he's a murderer, too. After Derrick meets with Kiel and gets paid for the hit, let's get some search warrants together and knock on a few doors."

~

As they sat huddled around the digital camera looking into the view finder at a secluded table in the rear of the Claim

Jumper, Kiel smiled at his co-conspirators and said, "It's so sad when these tragic accidents happen," and then added, "Now hit delete." He handed Derrick an envelope of cash. "Good job! We all feel a little better now. He was a douche bag anyway."

CHAPTER 23: THE ROUNDUP

Even though Kiel felt relief that Kurt "Jessie" James was no longer a threat, he still had an unexplainable gnawing feeling that something was wrong. He had spent a lifetime as a career criminal and with that had developed a keen sense for self-preservation. All successful predators in the food chain had to have it if they were to survive. He wasn't any different. In fact, he was better at it than most. He had learned to listen to his instincts and not ignore them. He retraced his steps from his first day of being placed here by the witness protection program. Was there some hole he didn't plug? Was there somebody he trusted that he shouldn't have? Did he fuck somebody over that he shouldn't have? Of course he did. It's what he did! He smiled to himself.

Maybe it was time to make the call to the U.S. Marshal's Office and set the stage to move on, just in case. He had diverted some of the investors' funds into a separate account in his secretary's name, which she didn't know about, and left enough clues for any prying investigator to find if it came to that. She would take the fall and attention would be diverted from him to her once the evidence was found. If all else failed, he had several of the tapes that he had recorded of some of the extortionate demands made by the corrupt Esmeralda County official, his "best friend." He would trade the information and set him up and testify against him if it came to that. He'd done it before and he'd do it again in a heartbeat. It was always good to have something that those asshole government prosecutors wanted as an ace in the hole. After thinking about it for a while, he was satisfied that even if he had made a mistake, he could still fix it. It was too easy. He was gifted!

~

"Deputy U.S. Marshal Castro speaking, how can I help you? Hi, Kiel. Is everything okay up there? Let me contact the relocation unit and find out what's available. No promises except that I'll look into it." The monitoring agent recorded the call.

~

"The only decision to make is whether we execute search warrants and make arrests at the time of the searches, or do the search warrants only and let the wiretap go on for a short period of time. The advantage is that by not arresting, we may be able to capture additional incriminating conversations when panic sets in before they realize that the phone is tapped. Plus we don't have to rush the investigation. There's still a lot more work that has to be done on this." The Assistant U.S. Attorney pondered.

Matt jumped in. "Given the fact that Kiel has already set the stage for leaving town and his propensity for violence, witnessed by his eager involvement in the Jessie James murder-for-hire plot, I think we should arrest him. He's a flight risk and he's dangerous." Matt looked around the room. Everyone there, including the prosecutor, was nodding their collective heads in agreement.

"The only thing is, I want the grand jury to indict on this matter, and we still have a lot of investigation that needs to be done. Subpoenas need to be served, accounts need to be reviewed, and a lot of out-of-state victim interviews need to be conducted. When we arrest, the clock is running under the speedy trial act, and we're not ready for that." The Assistant U.S. Attorney countered.

Charlie added, "Then why don't we do a complaint for his arrest on just one count, something that don't need any out-of-state victim interviews or records that don't need to be reviewed? We can indict them later on all of the other fraud counts. Let's arrest them for the murder plot. We've got everything we need on that." The decision was made.

The night before the raid, Alex pulled Matt away from Charlie. "Please don't ask me why or any other questions about it, but when you are helping out the task force tomorrow, if you see a building like a faded blue painted garage or an old barn that has a faded white number 142 on it, if you can go into it, go into a back room. It should have a lot of junk in it." She described the building and room from her recent dream. She continued, "In the southeast corner of the room dig around the area and see if there is anything there. Whatever you find, bring it back to me."

Matt was astounded at her request. "Alex I don't know where you're going with this, but I've known you long enough to know that you wouldn't ask me to do this unless it was important. Whatever reason you have for this, it's your business, and I won't ask you why. If I see the place that you've described, I'll do what you've asked."

One of the great advantages that the FBI had over local and state law enforcement agencies was the fact that the Bureau could pick the most strategic time and place to affect an arrest. Because most subjects of a federal investigation had been under the scrutiny of a wiretap or some other form of surveillance, the agents could calculate when they would be most likely to get the evidence that they needed, and the safest time to do it. Usually it was just before dawn, when the bad guys were sleeping off a hangover. This case wouldn't be any different.

~

"FBI! Open the door! We have a search warrant," the SWAT team leader commanded. Shortly thereafter Kiel's beautiful front door almost came off its hinges as the ram piloted by the two huge FBI SWAT team members plowed into it. Next came the "flash bang" explosions and the team shouted their presence as they cleared each room and made their way into the bedroom. When they encountered him, Kiel was hiding under the bedspread with tears streaming down his face.

"Please don't hurt me! I'll do anything you ask! Just don't hurt me!" He pleaded. He was placed under arrest by George Lyford and read the Miranda warning. When George read the arrest warrant to him, he identified him only as Kiel Sandefur. Sandefur responded to the case agent, now getting his confidence back somewhat. "I don't think you know who you are dealing with agent."

George fired back. "Yes, I do, Mr. Lionel Blanchard." Kiel was crushed.

The raid and search warrant at the Esmeralda County official's residence wasn't as dramatic, because of his wife and children. It always pained George and the other agents to take a man into custody in front of his children. It would be an event that could traumatize them, so no forced entry was made. Instead, there was a knock on the door.

Search warrants were also served at the Macsvog International office, several Nevada State Bank safety deposit boxes, and the Esmeralda County Recorders Office. All together, over two million dollars in cash was seized along with books, receipts, telephone records, and three ounces of cocaine that Kiel had in his nightstand. He would be charged with possession as well.

Just to get everything they could out of Derrick's cooperation, they equipped him with a recorder and placed him in the jail cell along with the other two, and made it appear that he was under arrest as well. They were at each other's throats with blame and further incriminating conversations which would all be admissible in court.

"How did they find out that we had him killed?" The county official asked both Kiel and Derrick.

"Shut the fuck up. We don't want them to get any more evidence on us. It's bad enough that they know we had it done." Kiel admonished him.

~

Now that Matt was a private citizen, he had no legal right to assist the agents in their search. In fact, if he did assist them and some critical piece of evidence was found, it could be a point of contention with the defense, so he just stood on the sidelines while the searches were being conducted. While the agents conducted the search of the county official's residence in Goldfield, he waited outside the house, and began looking around the area just to kill time. The public official and his extended family had occupied the home and surrounding buildings since the old days. That's when he saw it … just the way Alex had described it!

The number 142 painted on a faded light blue building nearby that looked like an old garage or barn. There were several chickens hanging around the front of the building pecking at the ground. It was surreal. How could she know? Had she been here before? He decided to follow through with his promise to Alex and went inside. He saw a room in the back of the building full of old boxes and junk, just as she said he would find. As directed, he walked to the southeast corner of the room and looked around and didn't see anything. He took the heel of his boot and began kicking away at the dirt floor near the corner. The dirt was compacted and hard, so he found a piece of metal pipe and began to dig in the area. After digging into the hard dirt about six inches deep, he hit something metal. It was a square box about six inches by six inches. Whatever was inside had been there for a long time. He left the building without saying anything to anyone.

The search warrants and accompanying interviews took the rest of the day for the task force to complete, and Matt didn't return back to Pigeon Spring until well after dark. Charlie headed back to Las Vegas. When Matt got back, Alex was waiting up for him.

She met him out on the front porch with a light kiss and a warm lingering hug. She thought about the many road trips and undercover assignments they had endured in the past and was always glad and relieved when this moment came. She hoped this was the last one, but she thought that she had seen the last of it when he retired, too.

"I gather everything went okay?'

"Better than okay. It went just as planned. What a swan song. I think we did something good today."

"I hope it was a swan song, but somehow I don't think that you've hung up your spurs yet, cowboy. Did you find anything for me?" He handed her the unopened box. She smiled at her husband and best friend and they went inside.

The next morning, Alex woke Matt up after she fed the horses. "Matt I know what I'm supposed to do. Come with me." She was excited and couldn't wait to do what she was compelled to do. Matt got dressed and followed her out. She had the metal box he had retrieved from the old workshop under her arm. He followed her down the path toward the stamp mill and then east on the old logging road. When she got to the gravesite, she stopped, and for the first time opened the metal box. Matt was shocked at what he saw.

Alex asked, "What was the name of the Esmeralda County official that your task force arrested?" She was staring intently at the box's contents.

"His name is Wallace Stow ... Wallace Stow III. His great-grandfather was one of the local characters from this area ... a notorious prospector and infamous drunk."

With that she reverently removed the unbelievably huge gold nugget from the box, and with Matt's help, they buried it deep next to Nancy Walker's grave. It had been hers and she had paid for it with her life. Now it was hers again.

CHAPTER 24: THE AFTERMATH

To say that Sandefur and Wallace Stow were shocked was a vast understatement when at the preliminary hearing they learned that Derrick had been cooperating with the authorities for some time. But when they saw Jessie James alive, cleaned up, and walking into the courtroom they were bewildered beyond description. When the defense attorney was informed at the preliminary hearing that both of them would be testifying against his clients, he wanted to cut an immediate plea deal. Eventually the government would negotiate an agreement, but not just now. The Assistant U.S. Attorney would let them sweat for a while and thereby broker a more favorable plea agreement for the government. It would include restitution for some of the elderly victims and lengthy prison sentences for both of them. The ensuing investigation revealed that Kiel had victims all over the country numbering in the hundreds. He had taken the life savings from the sick and old, from the educated and uneducated, from the rich and made them poor, from the poor and made them poorer. His was the cruelest of crimes. It left a legacy of broken hearts, divorces, separated families, and four suicides. And he did this all under the nose of the Witness Protection Program.

The wiretap revealed that Stow was also on the take with three other large mining companies, basically doing the same thing as he was doing with Kiel. Later, when he would cooperate with the government as part of his plea agreement, six of the mining company executives would enter guilty pleas for their part in the extortion and bribery schemes.

"Internal Affairs, Lieutenant Davis' office; how may I help you?" The secretary had an arrogance to her voice.

"Yes, is the Lieutenant in? This is Sergeant Marty Torgler from Organized Crime."

"Hold on. I'll see if he can receive your call." She put him on hold. Marty thought to himself, 'receive my call,' what kind answer is that? After a lengthy wait, Lt. Davis 'received' the call.

"What can I do for you, Sergeant?" He had a snotty condescending way about him. Marty decided to play him and assumed a subservient position in the conversation.

"Well sir, I wanted to try to contact that Deputy U.S. Marshal that I spoke with in your office. I've been thinking about things, and I want to tell him something. I thought maybe it might be best if we met in your office."

The Lieutenant smelled the humiliation in his voice and pounced on it. "I see, Sergeant. You've apparently been thinking about things. It's always best to come clean on these things. I've found that the truth eventually comes out anyway. I'll notify him that you wish to discuss this matter further. Let's meet in my office this afternoon, say around two o'clock."

"Yes sir."

Lt. Davis smirked as he hung up the phone. Another smart-assed cop would be getting what was coming to him.

Deputy U.S. Marshal Castro and Lt. Davis were already in Lt. Davis' office when he arrived. He could hear their muffled laughter just inside the office door. "Lieutenant Davis, the Sergeant is here," his uppity secretary announced. "Can you receive him now?"

Receive him? It was like he was some sort of office supply delivery, he thought. "Yes, send him in."

When he walked in, all of the laughter he had heard was now gone, replaced by stern and somber stares. "Of course you remember Deputy U.S. Marshal Castro, Sergeant." No offer of a handshake was made by either of them. "Take a seat." It was more of a command by the Lieutenant than a request. After he was seated, the deputy marshal stood up and looked down at him in a position of authority, ready to hear his admission of wrongdoing and misuse of his position. The Lieutenant especially enjoyed this moment: the split seconds just before a confession was made, and someone's life would be turned inside out. The practiced bully hid his glee.

"The Lieutenant tells me that you have something to tell me." The Deputy Marshal paused, waiting for Marty to make the next move.

"Well sir," he was trying to string it out as long as he could, "when we last met, I told you that I was working a case on that fellow up in Tonopah."

"Yes. Go on." The Deputy Marshal prodded. The Lieutenant was on the edge of his chair.

"I think I need to be more forthright with you regarding what I did. I didn't tell you the whole truth." Lieutenant Davis was practically licking his chops waiting for Marty's full confession about his misuse of his position. But what happened next was not in the Lieutenant's playbook.

"Well sir, it appears that your protected witness Kiel Sandefur aka Lionel Blanchard has been running a nationwide fraud scheme right under your nose and I have a federal grand jury subpoena commanding your appearance this Friday. The U.S. Attorney has a lot of questions as to how this could have happened under your watch. Please be on time. The grand jury convenes at nine o'clock promptly. And Lieutenant, the U.S.

Attorney said that he wouldn't subpoena you just yet, but wanted you to make yourself available just in case he needed to receive you later." Actually the U.S. Attorney didn't say that, but Marty couldn't help himself.

Marty thought that the Deputy Marshal was going to faint. All the color drained from his face and he had that deer-caught-in-the-headlights look about him. Lieutenant Davis' response was even more revealing. When he saw the subpoena being handed to the deputy marshal, he physically stepped back, and for a moment, Marty thought he was going to run out of his own office. The moment was priceless! "Thank you gentlemen. See you on Friday, Mr. Castro. And Lieutenant, if you are going to be out of town, let me know where I can reach you."

~

During the search of the Esmeralda County Recorders Office, the original paperwork for the claim by R&R Mining was found under a set of records in a drawer of an unoccupied desk in a back room. Now Red and Raymond could go on with the final step in filing the claim: the state survey. It was a mere formality, but before it could be officially theirs, it had to be completed.

Red and Raymond went back to the claim and after cleaning up the litter from its former occupants, re-established themselves there. They decided that the first thing to do would be to set up an office at the mining site and get someone to stay there as a watchman. Old Red had an elderly cousin who would be perfect for the job. Like Red, he was somewhat of a hermit, too. He looked a lot like old Red as well — tall and a thick head of red hair with a smattering of gray. Ray had an old camper trailer that would do just fine as the office and the old man would find it comfortable enough.

~

When George Lyford was driving back to the FBI office in Las Vegas, his Bureau car was packed to the roof with boxes of evidence from the day's searches. He couldn't even see out of the back window from the rearview mirror. But he did see something! It was something that would go straight to Kiel's intent to defraud his victims, and it demonstrated his extreme disrespect for his sponsor, the United States government. As George looked at the reversed image of one of the boxes in the back seat with the company label facing him, he saw it: govscam! Macsvog spelled backward was Govscam! What an arrogant, mocking, sociopathic scumbag this guy was. He would be sure that it was used against him in court. He would make certain of it.

CHAPTER 25: BACK TO NORMAL
SORT OF

The juvenile red-tailed hawks were now ready to venture out on their own. They spent the summer and fall learning how to live and survive independently. The young raptors had acquired and inherited all the necessary tools that they would need to flourish. Their attentive parents had taught them how to fly, hunt, attack, retreat, and socialize. They would stay around for a little while longer before they separated from their paternal guidance. It was a time of uncertain anticipation for them all. Alex hoped that the cycle would not be broken by events unseen or unpredicted. In the meantime she enjoyed their majesty and grace.

When Matt returned back to work at the casino, he was buried for two days just following up on the several hundred emails that had accumulated and reviewing paper work that required his signature. This was the only part of his new career that he didn't like. Nevertheless, it was part of the job, so he did his best. The second night he worked late just to get caught up and didn't leave the casino until around 8:00 p.m.

As he was leaving, he noticed a couple of hookers walking down the street in front of the casino. They were not on the property, so he couldn't do much about it except make it uncomfortable for them to be hanging around. When he got complaints about them from guests, he would instruct his outside units to sit in the area where they were walking and turn on the overhead emergency lights on the security patrol vehicles. They didn't want the undue attention, and would usually move on. Every time the vice unit put a push on them down on the Strip, it forced them in the direction of his casino. This was one of those challenging shades of gray that he struggled with. After all, this was Sin City, and he wasn't the moral police. But he did encourage the vice unit to come in and work his property. He provided them with rooms to conduct their stings and anything else they needed. Matt knew that if he ignored the prostitution problem, it would get a foothold, and when that happened, other crimes would take root as well. Trick rolls, purse snatchings, drugs, and muggings were all part of it, so when he saw the trend heading that way, he took action. He would meet with his supervisors the next day and get a game plan together. He would also call Metro and ask for some assistance from the vice unit.

"Hello, Chief. Sorry to wake you up so early. This is Sergeant Morris from graveyard shift."

Matt looked at the clock on the nightstand. It was 3:21 a.m. "Yeah, Scott; What's up?" Matt rubbed the sleep from his eyes as his graveyard shift supervisor briefed him on the shooting. "I'll be there is a few minutes."

"Is everything all right?" Alex asked, still groggy from sleep.

"No, we just had a shooting in a hotel room. I've got to go."

When he arrived at the casino, Matt went straight up to room 1034 where the dispatcher said the shooting had taken place. He had his Sigsauer 9mm on his side, just in case it wasn't all over. It was highly unlikely, but experience had taught him to expect the unexpected. When he arrived, he saw Sergeant Morris and several of his security officers standing outside the room along with a Metro lieutenant in uniform and a couple of plainclothes detectives. He didn't know the lieutenant, but he recognized one of the detectives, Dick Tomasso. Matt had worked with him briefly on a task force several years before. He always enjoyed his sense of humor, and like Matt, he hated motorcycle cops. It just didn't seem like real police work to him, and they seemed to enjoy their job a little too much, so he busted their balls whenever he could. Matt remembered once when he and Tomasso, both in plain clothes, stopped at a Starbucks for a cup of coffee. Sitting near the front of the coffee shop were two motorcycle officers, who apparently didn't know Tomasso. When they walked in, Tomasso looked at both officers and announced loud enough for anyone nearby to hear: "So what do we have here? It looks like a couple of *misdemeanor* cops in a *felony* world." One of the officers was so rattled that he spilled his coffee all over his tan pants and down into one of his shiny black Gestapo boots. Matt could see that they were really pissed and wanted a piece of him.

"Relax fellas'. I'm just bustin' your chops," and he flashed his badge and ID to them.

"Hey Matt. I heard you came over here as the chief of security after you retired, but I haven't had a chance to stop by and say hi. I guess this is a little more than a social call." Tomasso reached out and clasped Matt's hand with both of his.

"What's the deal here, Dick? How's the victim?" He could see blood splattered all over the walls and door, and a pool of blood soaking into the carpet near the room entrance.

"He's at UMC in extremely critical condition. He might not make it. He took a nine millimeter to the abdomen." Matt could see that one of the officers was interviewing a thin white male inside the room. He looked like he was in his early to mid-thirties. He had blood smeared all over his face and neck, and his shirt was torn.

"What's the deal with him?" Matt asked, motioning toward the white male.

"He's the buddy of the victim. They're both in town from Youngstown, Ohio, celebrating the victim's 40th birthday. It looks like they met a couple of hookers down in one of the casino bars and negotiated a love fest. After they got up to the room, one of the ladies said she had to leave. The other one said that her sister was down in the casino, and she would get her to come up to the room. She got the room key from the victim and met with her pimp. It seems that these guys were flashing a lot of money around so they decided to rob them. The hooker and the pimp came back to the room, and after gaining entry, he pulled his weapon and tried to rob them. What he didn't know was that both the victim and his buddy were highly trained in the marshal arts, and they proceeded to kick the livin' shit out of the pimp. When the hooker saw that they were getting the best of him, she jumped into the mix and the pimp was able to retrieve his weapon and get one shot off, and they both fled. We think they went down the stairwell. One of your officers found a bloodied shirt in the stairwell on the floor below us. They said that they busted him up pretty good," and Tomasso pointed to two teeth on the floor mixed in with the blood.

Matt turned to Sergeant Morris. "What do we have from surveillance?"

"They're working on it right now. They should have something for us any minute. They think they have a good facial of the pimp, and they're backtracking his movements in the casino. As soon as we get any footage, we'll get it to the detectives."

"How about other guests on the floor? How have you dealt with them?" Matt needed to brief the general manager, and he knew this would be one of his questions.

"Several called it into security dispatch when they heard the gunshot. We told them that everything was all right and that we are investigating it. Two of them insisted that they heard an unmistakable gunshot sound, and demanded to know what was going on. We stuck to our general story and upgraded their rooms on another floor. We also comped them to a show in the showroom and bought them dinner in the steakhouse for tonight. They forgot about being upset about the incident."

"Good job, Scott. I'm going to call the GM."

After Matt briefed the general manager and corporate security/risk management, he and Tomasso met in the coffee shop.

"Matt, I think we should be able to solve this one. There's a lot of DNA laying around the room, and I've gotta think that this guy has a rap sheet as long as my arm. The surveillance photo from the elevator isn't as good as I had hoped it would be. The pimp turned away from the full view of the camera, but we got a fairly decent side shot of him. We got a better shot of both of the females. I'm thinking that when the one got wind of what the other one had in mind, she backed out and didn't want any part of it."

"We'll have surveillance continue to backtrack with whatever footage they can get of him. Maybe we'll get some better shots," Matt offered.

"How much longer are you going to be doing this cop stuff? Shouldn't you be eligible to retire soon? You know there is a life after retirement. If you can find a gig like this, it's a perfect fit for a guy like you."

"Oh yeah. It's easy for you to say that. You feds get all the good jobs. All we locals get are the leftovers that you guys don't want." Tomasso laughed.

~

When Ernie answered the phone he did so with a non-committal "yeah."

"You sound like you don't want to talk to me. What's wrong? Did you think it was somebody trying to collect a debt?"

"Matt! I thought maybe you forgot me. Remember, I'm the guy who made you a superstar," and he laughed the gruff laugh of a lifetime as a mobster.

When Matt first met him in Detroit twenty years earlier, it was right after he beat the triple homicide case against him. The timing was just right, and Ernie was vulnerable for recruitment as a highly-placed confidential source for the Bureau. Ernie beat the case on a defense of self-defense, and the jury bought it. And they should have, too. The first time they met, it was in the back room of Ernie's brother John's restaurant.

"Ernie, the case is over now and you can't be retried on it. From what I read in the paper, it was a set up, but tell me what happened."

The pitch must have hit the right note, because Ernie opened up. Mostly he did so because he was pissed that he was double-crossed, and he realized that he had enemies out there and wasn't sure who they were. He might need a guy like Matt.

Matt knew this informant business was a curious balancing act for both parties. If Matt went too fast with Ernie, it might turn him off and he would lose him. When Matt would finally get to the point in their relationship that he could ask Ernie substantive questions about issues involving organized crime, he would have to be careful not to give up more information than he got. Simply inquiring about somebody was giving up something, that the Bureau has an interest in that person. It was a risk that could compromise an investigation if it fell into the wrong hands. It was a risk for the informant as well. What if somebody found out that they were talking? It could be deadly. These guys lived on the streets. They had to have instincts that the rest of society didn't, just to survive. They could pick up on a look in the eye or the subtle verbal cues of a lie that were invisible to law-abiding folks. Even a person's absence could be interpreted the wrong way.

"Well, it all started when Balls Belloti came into my crap game and wanted me to pay tribute. I told him to go fuck himself. I didn't have to pay nobody but the cops. I knew he was acting on his own, and Jackie T. didn't sanction it. He was pissed, but after a couple of months he acted like he forgot about it and I went on as usual. Then one day Frankie Randoza, who I knew since I was twelve, met with me and said that he was doing an insurance job on a safe and wanted to stash it in my basement. He said he would give me a couple of thousand if he could leave it there for a month or two. I said sure. What the fuck? But I had a funny feeling about it. I don't know why. So about a week later Frankie calls me and says he's got the safe and would I meet him at my house to help him move it. When I got there he was there waitin' for me. I helped him get the safe out of the trunk of his car and we brought it into the back door of the house. When we were takin' it down the steps to the basement, I tried to turn on the basement light, and it didn't work. We got to the bottom of the stairs and I could hear Frankie breathing real heavy-like. I knew we should be breathin' harder, but not that hard. All off a sudden he grabs me from the back and pins my arms down to my sides and yells, "I got him. I got him." Then Joe Spinelli jumps out and starts stabbing me in the chest with an ice pick, and swearing at me in Italian, but after he stuck me a couple of times he stuck Frankie in the hand and he let go of me for a second. I can't believe what's goin' on, and to make it worse, this motherfucker Belloti, takes a .38 with a towel wrapped around it and points it at my head and pulls the trigger. The dumb fuck didn't know it, but the towel was in between the hammer and the firing pin and it didn't go off. About this time, I'm able to pull my pistol out of my belt, and I go bingo, bango, bongo, and get all three. I'll tell you Matt; I was so scared that I didn't even open the back screen door. I just ran through it. I got in my car and drove myself to the hospital and called the cops. After I told them what happened, they arrested me for triple homicide. The motherfuckers!"

Ernie was a top-level mob informant from that moment on. Throughout the following years he helped bring down the hierarchy of the mob in Detroit, Cleveland, and Milwaukee, and nobody ever found out that he was involved. Ernie got his revenge. When Matt transferred to the Las Vegas Division of the FBI, he got a call from Ernie a couple of months later. "Hey Matt, me and Violet sold the house and moved to Vegas. Got any work for me out here?" He followed Matt. It was a tribute to their perverse twisted relationship.

"Ernie. I need to run something by you. Can you meet me at Capo's for a drink tonight?"

"So you still need your old friend, huh? I'll see if I can clear my calendar. I'll see you at six o'clock."

Ernie loved to meet at Capo's. The Italian restaurant and bar was a knock-off of an old Chicago speakeasy, complete with the hidden greeting door where the host, a gruff unsavory-looking character named Dominic playing the role of a mobster would open the peep door and say, "What d'ya want?" And the really good thing about the place was that no real wise guys went there. It was a perfect meeting place. They had great food as well.

"How's Violet? I still don't know what she ever saw in you. How many years has it been now?" Matt gave his old Bureau source a hug.

"She always told me that she liked the bad boys, and I was the baddest of them all." Ernie laughed. "In January, we'll be married forty-seven years." They both ordered a glass of Chianti.

"I gotta tell you, Matt, I sure miss the old days. I tried to work with those new guys you hooked me up with, but it just wasn't the same. I mean they're nice guys, but I don't know. We just didn't click."

"Don't worry about it, Ernie. Believe me. The contributions you made in the past were more than anybody else I ever met. You kicked some serious ass. It's time to pass the torch. Let it go. Enjoy life. It's time to relax."

"Yeah, just like you are doin': Relaxin.' "Now what the fuck brings us together tonight?" Matt briefed him on the shooting in the hotel room. They ordered some calamari and another glass of wine.

~

When Ray got the official letter from the Nevada State Office of the Bureau of Land Management, he couldn't wait to open it. It would be the survey statement and the final step in the long hard-fought battle to establish R & R Mining. He decided to drive over to Red's place and open it there. Maybe they would celebrate with a glass of old Red's peach brandy. On the way over, Ray thought about the budding new enterprise and the good things it might bring to all of them. He never envisioned himself in this position. Life was funny. Just a year or so earlier, he and Linda were barely scratching out a living doing intermittent dozer work and cowboying whenever he could. And old Red was pecking around the hills like an old rooster looking for chicken scratch. And now here they were, sitting on one of the most promising shows there ever was in this part of the country. It was a good feeling.

"Well, what are you waitin' for, Ray? Open up the letter! I'll get the brandy." Red belted out as he opened the nearby cabinet and reached for his jug.

As Ray looked at the official state stationary, he saw the words, but he didn't comprehend what he was reading, and it took almost a complete paragraph before he understood.

"Pursuant to Nevada law (NRS 517.213; NAC 517.160 it is required that the County Recorder include all patented mines and mining claims on the county map and clearly distinguish them from unpatented claims. When a registered surveyor files a record of survey showing the location of a patented mine or mining claim, the County Recorder must conform the county map to the record of survey, if there is any discrepancy between the two. Accordingly, our records have determined that your claim, as submitted as R & R Mining Inc. cannot be recognized by the State of Nevada, inasmuch as the location of said enterprise, as identified in the supporting documents previously provided by R & R Mining Inc., is located entirely on privately held property. The 20-acre placer claim in west, northwest quarter, northwest quarter 16, T28N, R56E, is privately held by the Timbisha Shoshone Tribe as authorized by the Timbisha Homeland Act of November 1st, 2000.

Should you have any questions regrding. these findings please ..."

Raymond put the letter down without reading anymore.

The young red-tailed hawks left. Maybe they would return someday

CHAPTER 26: OBSTACLES

"Matt. We're not having much luck with our informants in the vice unit. I think somebody out there knows who it is, but for whatever reason, they're not talking. I think the pimp might be a gang-banger and everybody is intimidated. The only good thing so far is that it looks like the victim is going to make it. It was touch and go for him for a couple of days, and they had to do a temporary colostomy on him, but the doctor said that if infection doesn't set in, he should be all right." Tomasso briefed Matt on the status of the hotel shooting. "We're waiting for DNA tests to come back from the lab. Maybe we'll get something out of that."

"Thanks Dick. I've got to keep upper management in the loop here, so I appreciate the update." Matt hung up the phone.

~

"What'd you want?" Dominic, the would be gangster, answered the door.

"I really like that. It reminds me of the old days." Ernie laughed his graveled laugh as he was let into Capo's by the doorman. Matt was already sitting at a dimly-lit table in the back of the room up on the elevated dining area behind where the nightly crooner Bobby Liguori did a fairly good Sinatra routine. The ladies loved him.

"I took the liberty of ordering you a glass of Chianti." Matt motioned for Ernie to take a seat.

"Great! I need it. I took the points on the Steelers game, and they got killed. They didn't even come close to the spread … the motherfuckers."

The singer, Bobby, didn't know who Ernie was, though he grew up on 18th Street, not far from the organized crime bastion of Mulberry Street in New York City, and he had spent a lot of time around real wise guys, so he knew instinctively that Ernie had a background. Accordingly, he was more than gracious in greeting him. Ernie loved the attention.

"Hey it's great to see you again! You got any special requests?"

"No kid. Just keep doin' the Sinatra thing. I really like it."

"You bet," and he did a resounding rendition of "My Kind Of Town," occasionally smiling with a nod toward Ernie. Ernie turned to Matt and said, "The kid's not bad."

"Listen Matt, I think I got something for you. You know those leaflets that those bums pass out on the strip? You know, the ones with all the half-naked girls on the front ... the ones that say, "College girls direct to your hotel room and all that shit?"

"Yeah, it's just a front for prostitution," Matt acknowledged.

"Right. Well, I know this guy from LA who's involved in it. We were talking about the problems he's been havin' with some of these girls' pimps. I think he was lookin' for some muscle help from somebody like me to straighten it out. So we're talkin' and I say something like ... these motherfuckers are gettin' brave, and I mention something about the shooting at your hotel. He tells me he's been having problems with this same guy who did the shooting, and says that he wants me to have a talk with him. The pimp's name is Stancil Williams, also known as "Stan the Man." He's with the Crips. He stays with a couple of his girls over at the Budget Suites on west Tropicana. So I tell my guy that first I'll have a conversation with this guy I know who is in charge of him, and see if that changes his attitude."

"Ernie; you are the man!" Matt was elated. "Now where's my calamari?" Ernie grinned at his old contact agent.

~

When the SWAT team hit room 2015 at the Budget Suites at 6:00 a.m. the next morning, Stan the Man was in bed, naked and sound asleep, with one of the girls involved in the shooting. She flippedon him during questioning and identified the other prostitute also involved. The search team found about two ounces of cocaine in a gym bag in the closet, and a nine-millimeter Glock under the bed. Later, ballistics linked the weapon to the round that was taken out of the victim. When the DNA test results came back from the lab, Stan the Man's cells were identified as being all over the hotel room. He would be gone for a long time.

CHAPTER 27: THE STRUGGLE

Joe Gonzalez sat in the tribal counsel open meeting and listened to the elders retrace their battle for their heritage. He had heard about it many times in the past, but he knew that in order for the younger generation to carry on the struggle after the older ones were gone, the past had to be seared into their minds.

The land of the Timbisha Shoshone *was* their identity, and for 150 years, they lost it: the soaring mountain peaks, the springs, and pinion pines, the mesquite trees, the deer and jackrabbits, the big horn sheep, and lizards. When the Timbisha came to this place thousands of years ago, this land provided them with all of their needs. For eons they hunted, gathered for sacred dances, and listened to the storytellers. They collected plants for eating and healing. The women made baskets, and the men made bows and arrows. They were people of the earth. Even their name "Timbisha" symbolized their intimacy with nature. It meant "red rock face paint."

After he completed his course of carpentry study at the Indian school in Idaho, Joe got a job in Las Vegas building houses with one of the large developers. He had never lived in a big city before and was totally unprepared for it. He began drinking too much and gambling too much, and predictably started to get into trouble with the law. One night when he found himself in the Clark County Detention Center sleeping off a drunken night of disorderly conduct, Joe Gonzalez took a hard look at the direction his young life was headed and made a

U-turn. He went back to Fish Lake Valley where he was from. That was five years ago. Since then he married Relinda, the Navajo girl he met at the Idaho school, and he was the proud father of a two-year-old boy. It was tough to make a decent living in Fish Lake Valley, but he had a good reputation as a hard worker, as well as a skill, so the locals gave him work when they could. This was his home, and this is where his people were.

He was at the tribal meeting because he had ignored his heritage too long. He realized that if the young people of the tribe didn't take an interest in who they were and where they were from, they were destined to lose it again. He didn't want to be a leader. He only wanted to become part of it. So he listened respectfully to the elders tell their story to those who sat in the meetinghouse.

"When we helped the lost white people who came to our valley a hundred and fifty years ago from the east, the word spread to others. They saw what we had, and soon they came here to build ranches and mine for gold and silver. Our springs were taken from us. Our pinions were cut down and our way of life changed. We couldn't live off of the land like our fathers before us lived. We found other ways to live and provide for our families. We cut firewood, and worked on their ranches and in their mines. Our women did laundry in the towns. We became guides and message carriers. We did what we had to do to survive. Some fought back, and there were hostilities between the whites and the Shoshone and our brothers, the Paiutes. Then in 1866 the Treaty of Ruby Valley was signed. It was a statement of friendship and allowed white people to safely cross our land. Some of our women even married some of the white men and they had families. Even so, many of the

Anglos misunderstood the Native American culture and our values and sometimes there was tension. Our hunting areas continued to be taken by them. Then in 1936, the Conservation Corps built nine adobe homes and a trading post for us and gave us only forty acres of land at Furnace Creek. For a long time we had no voice. Then in 1983 we got recognition as a true tribe. Our lives began to get a little better. We got electricity and some paved roads. Then in 1994 the California Desert Protection Act was signed into law by President Clinton. The law said that the government had to find lands suitable for a real reservation in our homelands. When the National Park Service told the tribe that there was no "suitable" land for a reservation here, we went to the media. The media became our friend and stronger than any tribe of Native Americans ever was. On November 1st, 2000, the Timbisha Homeland Act was signed into law, and to right the wrongs that were done to us, we were given back 7,500 acres of land in California and Nevada."

"Why do we always bring this up at open meetings?" Henry Ritchie, the elder looked directly at Joe when he asked the question, so Joe answered for all of the others.

"We are told this so we will never forget how we lost our land and never allow ourselves to let this happen again."

The elder said, "Joe, please stand up before everyone and say that again, only say it louder so they can all hear the answer." So Joe stood up before the group of Timbisha and did as requested. Henry thanked Joe, and repeated Joe's statement just for emphasis. "We will never let this happen again!"

~

Even though it was a bright and clear late fall day, there was an uncharacteristic feeling of gloom at Pigeon Spring. Matt and

Alex were up for the weekend and Red and Raymond were there giving them the bad news about the claim.

"Matt, when I opened the letter and read it, I didn't understand what I was reading. I mean, I understood the words, but they didn't register."

"I'll tell you what. After all we've been through, what with those swindlers and such, I still can't believe that we can't work that claim." Red was brokenhearted. "I knowed I couldn't have any kind of good luck." The old tall redhead actually looked like he had gotten a little shorter.

"Come on in for dinner." Alex took him by the arm and walked him and Raymond into the cabin. Matt followed.

Dinner that night was Charlie's hobo stew. He made a batch for Matt and Alex to take up to the ranch. Even though it was one of their favorites, Red and Raymond just didn't seem to have much of an appetite. As they sat around the fireplace that night after dinner, they discussed their options.

Matt inquired. "Are you sure that the property's legal description is accurate? Maybe there is some sort of mistake."

"Matt, that's the first thing I checked out. There's no mistake. I even went into the county recorders office, and doublechecked it myself. The land was deeded to the Timbisha as part of that Homeland Act back in 2000. Do you remember Joe Gonzales? He helped us when we were building the cabin."

"Yeah. He's a real nice kid and a hard worker, too." Matt noted.

"Well, he's been pretty active the last couple of years with the tribe, so I even had him meet with me and Red. He brought up a detailed map of the Timbisha land with him. There's no doubt. The claim is on their property."

Alex offered, "Maybe R & R Mining could lease the land

from them, or form some sort of partnership with them."

Red added, "We talked about that, but why would they need us? They could do it all themselves now that they know there's gold there. Even Joe said that they had to fight so hard to get the land back that the elders would never do anything like that. And they don't naturally like miners anyway. What with the way they tore up the land in the past and ran off all the Indians."

"There's got to be something that can be done," Alex said.

"Well, we're all ears if you can figure something out. That is, everyone except old Red." In spite of things, Raymond managed a peevish grin at his old hard hearing partner.

Red retorted. "I kinda' heard that." It was good to see that even under the current circumstances they were still able to muster up some humor. They would get through this, Matt thought.

~

"I could stay awake all night and watch you breathing" ... as Alex walked south through the valley between "Crow Chase" and another Mt. Magruder foothill she called Lost Cabin, she lightly sang the lyrics from "I Don't Want To Miss Anything," the 1980s hit song by Aerosmith. She was out the next morning following up on her obsession looking for artifacts. Woman Looks Down named the foothill after the old rock remains of a prospector's cabin from a bygone era that sat at the tip of a rock outcropping near the top. Like most of the ruins in these areas, the ever-present nearby trash dump held a wealth of information about the lives of those who lived there. Mostly there was just a pile of rusted out cans and broken glass, but occasionally she would find something that she didn't expect to

find, like the time she found the leg of a porcelain doll at one of these sites. This would have been rough living, even for a grizzled old prospector. Did a child live here as well? Or did he buy it for a daughter waiting back east for her father to return home flush with riches, but he never made it? She would never know.

The valley narrowed as Alex made her way, climbing higher toward Mt. Magruder. When she entered a thicket of pinions and juniper, she was startled to see two adult female mule deer along with a yearling standing a mere fifteen feet from where she stood, intently looking at her. Alex stopped her movement toward them, but continued with her rendition of the song. Instead of fleeing as expected, all three stood there with their noses sniffing the air and their elongated ears tilted in her direction. Alex continued lightly … *"Watch you smile while you are sleeping … While you're far away and dreaming. I could spend my life in this sweet surrender."* The two adult deer then did a remarkable thing; they took a few steps toward her … *"I could stay lost in this moment forever"* … When the yearling didn't step toward her as the adults did, the older ones stopped their advance. Alex continued. *"Every moment spent with you is a moment I treasure."* It was as if the deer were mesmerized by the sight of her along with the soothing lyrics she was lightly singing. She was sure that this must be their first encounter with a human. The curiosity about this strange being coupled with the soothing sound coming from it overrode their instincts to run. *"Don't want to close my eyes."* When the yearling continued her reluctance to follow the older ones, they all three gathered up and ran south. It was a moment to commit to her memory, and she repeated, *"Every moment spent with you is a moment I treasure."* Alex clutched the spearhead necklace hanging under her jacket.

She had been gone since mid-morning, and the western foothills were already casting the shadows of the late autumn setting sun. It was about 3:15 p.m. and she had about a forty-five minute hike back, give or take ten minutes. Matt would come looking for her if she didn't get back soon.

As Alex made her way back down the hillside and through the meadow, she thought she heard the faint sounds of the deer that she had encountered. Could it be that they were following her? That would be something else, she thought. She continued her route back toward Pigeon Spring, constantly listening for the deer behind her. Now the faint sound seemed to come from the densely forested hillside to the east of her. It wasn't even a sound really. It was more of a feeling than a sound. Sometimes the two senses overlapped, and one couldn't be separated from the other. There was something about it that she didn't quite feel comfortable with. It was difficult for her to explain, even to herself. It almost felt like she was being watched. If the deer were following her, they would be watching her as well, she reasoned. The feeling persisted. She didn't like it. This would be the feeling that the deer had when they were being watched by her. Were the deer following her? Or was it a predator like her? She did not consider herself a predator, but she was. Even though she would never kill, she was a predator. Yet sometimes the predator became the prey. Was she a predator or was she the prey? As the evening shadows grew longer, she quickened her pace.

Matt looked out from the west-facing cabin porch toward the setting sun. His concern for Alex began to grow. She should have been back by now. He holstered his 9 mm. Sigsauer on his side and headed down toward the corral. It took about five minutes to tack up the gelding palomino Brio, and when he did, he headed south past the spring and then east toward Mt. Magruder. He picked up Alex's foot tracks from earlier in the day and followed them up and over the ridge. She was more than capable of taking care of herself, but if she needed him, he would never forgive himself if he didn't go looking for her.

~

She heard something this time! It wasn't just a feeling. Something was following her! She saw the extra movement of the juniper limb about twenty yards to the east of her. She kept walking at her new pace. Now she was certain that it wasn't the deer. She stopped and picked up a pinion limb about the size of a large walking stick. She turned toward the sound and looked for movement, but didn't see any. She held the stick up and made herself look as big as she could. Her pulse quickened.

~

Matt lost the trail and circled around until he picked it up again. The trail meandered around a little and then continued heading east climbing another foothill. The mountain shadows grew longer. He was worried. He brought the horse up to a trot, but he lost Alex's footprints and had to stop more often. He would make better time if he slowed down and focused on the sometimes-light tracks. He continued east.

Alex felt warmth where the spearhead touched her chest, and she clasped the ancient relic hanging around her neck. At that instant when she was facing the poised unseen danger in front of her, a cloud breached the horizon behind her between the setting sun and her position. The sun, along with the rising cloud, cast her shadow into an image of a giant two-legged ogre with a mighty weapon in her hand on the hillside to the east. It was only for a moment or two, but it was enough. The 250-pound male mountain lion wanted no part of this horrific creature, and now he believed he might be the prey. He revealed himself and turned and ran much like the deer did earlier.

"Wo! OO! Wo! OO!" Matt called out. When he heard her call back he felt immediate relief. "I was getting a little worried. The sun is starting to set. It's not like it's summer out here anymore."

"I'm sorry, Matt. You know me. I just didn't realize how late it was getting."

"You don't need to apologize. I was just a little concerned that's all. I know you can take care of yourself. I'll pull up next to that log. Hop on and I'll give you a lift." Matt gave her a hand up they headed back to the ranch doubled up on Brio.

She kept silent about both encounters.

It was twilight when they got back. After he cleaned and brushed Brio, Matt fed the horses and headed back up to the cabin. Alex had already reheated the leftover stew and had a fire going in the fireplace. They had a glass of wine, sat by the fireplace and talked.

"It just seems so unfair that Red and Ray can't take ownership of the claim. All of his life, old Red has been looking for something like this, and now that he's found it, he can't have it. And poor Raymond and Linda; this would have been a blessing for them. What a disappointment. Maybe they should meet with the Timbisha anyway. What have they got to lose?" Alex didn't want them to give up.

"I don't know Alex. You heard Red say about how the tribe feels. They fought too long and hard to get some of their land back. They're not about to let any of it go back to the whites.

Not even in a business arrangement or any other kind of arrangement. This is their heritage. I just don't think there is anything that they can do."

"Maybe they can take on a Timbisha partner. Anyway, I think at least they should try to talk to them. The worst that they could say is no."

CHAPTER 28: GATHERING WOOD

As part of his newfound commitment to his community, Joe Gonzalez cut and gathered firewood for some of the elderly Timbisha living around Furnace Creek, Fish Lake Valley, and the northern part of Death Valley. He tried to do it every couple of weeks during the autumn months. After November, it was hit and miss running into bad weather in the mountains. The winter clouds tended to gather in the higher elevations this time of year and a storm could rush upon an unsuspecting traveler without notice. It could be sunny and clear down in the valley, but a snow squall could be raging at seven or eight thousand feet elevation.

He enjoyed seeing the faces of the older folks when he came to their modest homes unannounced with a load of wood. "Thank you Joe. We can't get out like we used to for the wood, and we didn't have enough money to buy any for the stove. We didn't know what we were going to do this year." It made him feel like he was helping out some folks who really needed it. They always offered him something for his efforts, but he rarely accepted anything. He took a chicken once, and a few eggs once or twice when it was offered, and he accepted a finely made basket one time when they really insisted. But he delivered the firewood just because he thought it was the right thing to do, and maybe someday someone might remember and do it for him when he couldn't cut wood anymore.

"I don't know, Relinda. There's some bad looking clouds over there near Sylvania. Maybe we should go a little further east toward Magruder. It looks a little clearer over there. Let's head up to Tule Canyon past Pigeon Spring. There's a lot of old pinion left over from the when the loggers were taking down the big pinions a long time ago near the old Klein Ranch." He always wondered why the loggers weren't more frugal, taking the smaller limbs, too. They were just about the right diameter for a stove or fireplace. He guessed that they probably took up too much room in the loggers' trucks and they weren't worth it to them. He was glad they didn't. It made it a lot easier for him.

When he took the turn off to Pigeon Spring from route 266 and made his way past the old stamp mill, he became excited as he neared the bend in the old stagecoach road and could see the cabin sitting up in the pine grove to the east. Even though it wasn't his, he took a lot of pride in the work he put into building it with Raymond and Matt. He remembered the big party they had when it was all finished. Matt said he was going to have some "dancing girls" there to celebrate. Matt's version of dancing girls was a lot different than his. It turned out that Matt's dancing girls were Linda, Alex, and Relinda, and they were doing more line dancing than anything else. It was a great time, though. The food, the country music, the beer, and peach brandy; it was the most noise at Pigeon Spring since Wovoka's ghost dance.

Matt was down by the corrals cleaning up the stalls when he saw Joe, Relinda, and their little son, Jeremiah, rounding the turn in their pickup. Matt smiled and waved to them. "How's things going? It's been months since I last saw you." Matt stopped what he was doing and greeted them by the ranch entrance.

"It's been a while. We've been down in Fish Lake Valley mostly. I've been getting a little work over at White Water

Ranch helping on building a couple of houses. They've just about sold all of the ten acre lots, and a few out-of-towners are starting to build."

"My God! What have you been feeding this kid of yours? He's doubled in size since I last saw him."

"He's getting good Indian food: jackrabbits, deer meat, and pine nuts," Joe laughed as he said it.

"Yeah, and he eats his share of Fruit Loops, too," Relinda added. "We're going up past the Klein Ranch to cut some firewood for the old folks. This'll probably the last time this season we can do it. We started to head out toward Sylvania, but it's looking kind of bad up there weather wise, so we thought we'd head up here instead."

"Well I'm glad you did. Why don't you guys stop for a while when you get back from cutting wood? I know Alex would love to see that little boy of yours."

"You bet. We'll see you later this afternoon," Joe responded.

When Alex got back from her daily walk, Matt told her about meeting Joe, Relinda, and little Jeremiah. "I'll bet he has grown like a weed since we last saw him. I love that dark hair and his little round face." Alex smiled as she described him.

"Well, you're going to be surprised when you see him. He's been doing a little growing the last few months. You won't believe how much."

~

When he got to the top of the meadow, about four miles south past Pigeon Spring on the old road toward Gold Point, Joe headed east on the faint ranch road toward the deserted Klein Ranch. It was a steep climb, so he shifted the truck into four-wheel drive. The Klein Ranch had once been a viable and profitable cattle operation, but it had been abandoned now for about seventy-five years. After the last resident died off, the Bureau of Land Management figured out that it was on federal land and nobody lived there since. A few buildings and corrals were still standing, although they were in a state of severe disrepair. An ancient lone apple tree remained standing guard at the entrance.

As they made their way up to the meadow and then down the next draw, Joe couldn't help but notice the never-ending signs of nature trying to balance herself. It was a constant push and pull: opposites attracting each other for the betterment of the whole. The mountain lion hated the coyote, but the lion would take the deer and leave the jackrabbit for the coyote. The jackrabbit would eat the plants, which would thrive on the carbon dioxide and droppings of the jackrabbits. Life was full of opposites and wouldn't be possible without them. Summer and winter, day and night, death and life — even man and woman. They were all opposites, and they all needed each other to achieve balance and thrive. He saw it when little Jeremiah was born and his elderly grandmother died two days later. He saw it now in the remaining flowers in the meadow, and the last of the few bees trying to extract the sparse late autumn drops of nectar, and unwittingly pollinating the next one. The deer droppings nourished the new flowers as the deer ate the mature ones. The never-ending tendency to balance between opposite forces was everywhere. You just had to look for it. It was part of the natural circle. Nature wanted to be round. He had learned to see this.

"Hey, it looks like you found the mother load." Matt was surprised to see how much cut wood they had gathered is such a short time. It seemed like they had been gone for only a couple of hours, but in fact, Joe and Relinda had been gathering pinion for most of the afternoon.

"Yep, we filled it up. It should keep a few old folks warm for a couple of days." Joe felt good with the pickup load behind him.

"Come on up to the cabin. I told Alex about how Jeremiah has grown, and she can't wait to see him. She's up there in the kitchen," Matt called out to Joe and Relinda from the corral. Joe pulled the pickup through the ranch gate, and Matt hoped onto the downed tailgate and motioned for him to drive up to the cabin.

When Alex heard the vehicle coming up the road, she walked out onto the front porch and waited for them. "Good Lord! Will you look at that boy? He's grown so much since the last time I saw him." Even though Matt had told her so, she didn't realize how much until she saw him herself. Relinda handed him to her when she got up to the porch. "I just love that little round face and his dark hair. "Alex smothered him with affection, but Jeremiah didn't seem to mind. In fact he laughed with all the attention Alex was bestowing on him.

"Hey, it's just about time for dinner. Can you guys stay and eat with us? Alex just made some chili and cornbread." Matt asked.

"We won't take no for an answer," Alex added.

"I guess we're staying for dinner then." Joe looked at Relinda, and she nodded in the affirmative.

After dinner, they all sat next to the fireplace, and Jeremiah played on the floor with some of the grandkids' toys. Joe and Matt tasted some of old Red's peach brandy. Alex and Relinda talked about raising kids.

"Have you talked with Ray or Red lately?" Matt asked.

"I saw them both down in Dyer the other day at the gas station. They're still pretty disappointed about the claim, but they seem to have accepted it. I feel real bad about it, and I hope they don't hate the Timbisha for it." Joe said. The conversation caught the attention of Alex.

"Joe, it just seems so unfair that they can't do something with that claim. I know that the Timbisha don't like miners, but sometimes opposing teams join together, and it works out better for everyone in the long run. Even enemies join forces sometimes. I mean we even had the Russians as allies during World War II. Without them, we all might be speaking German now. And there's no better people than Red and Raymond. If the tribe could just hear from them, they might change their minds. I think they all could profit from a joint venture. You know them. Is there any way that you could get the Elders to meet with them?"

Just then, little Jeremiah reached for the irresistible black spearpoint dangling from Alex's neck. She instinctively pulled back far enough so he couldn't reach it. "I don't think you're ready for that yet. It's powerful stuff."

Joe met Alex's eyes. It was powerful stuff. He could feel it. "Alex, all I can say is that I will ask for a meeting. The worst that can happen is that they say no." He thought about her choice of words, opposing teams.

CHAPTER 29: IMPROBABLE ALLIES

Swing shift supervisor Sergeant Alexander briefed him on the room break-ins as soon as Matt received the voicemail to call him when he got into cell phone range on the way back to Las Vegas. It became a more serious problem when Matt discovered that in each case, the master security override code was used to burglarize the room safes. Presumably, only the security shift supervisors and the field training officers had the code. Sergeant Alexander surmised from the tool marks on the room doors that the burglar may have used two prying instruments like a small crowbar or large screwdriver to gain entry into the rooms. One was used to pry the door out above the lock just enough to allow the second devise to be inserted to depress the lock plunger to gain entry. The burglar would have the perfect cover to conceal the tools, too: a suitcase or bag. Possession of a gym bag or suitcase wouldn't look unusual in a hotel setting. They had six rooms that were burglarized within two days, and whoever the thieves were went directly to the safes and used the security code to get into them. It was determined that the security code was used through the electronic interrogation of the safes. The device showed when entry was made and what code was used to gain entry.

Was it an inside job involving a bad security officer? Or did somebody else figure out the security code? It was conceivable that a would-be burglar could legitimately check into a room, use his individual code, lock his safe, and then call security and say that he forgot his code. If he could position himself in just the right spot, he might be able to glean a few of the digits from watching the security officer when he used the override code. Later, he could claim that he was drinking and forgot it again, and possibly get the rest of the code if he was lucky. He could also have an accomplice in another room who could do the same thing, and between them, they might be able to get the right code. More likely, though, it was somebody on the inside, but who could it be? Matt knew that only the security supervisors and the field training officers were the only ones who were supposed to have the code, but the reality of it was that people talked, even security personnel. Other employees could also get the code. Maybe someone in housekeeping observed it being used and over time was able to memorize it. The facilities engineers were always in the rooms, too, fixing things like toilets and changing lightbulbs. Maybe they could have gotten the code. It could even have been sold or passed on to an outsider. Matt had to terminate several employees over the past couple of years for misconduct. It could even be one of them. The possibilities were endless. To change the security override codes in all of the approximately two thousand safes with guests staying in the rooms twenty-four seven was a monumental task. The last time they changed the codes, it took about two weeks, and it was pretty disruptive to the guests.

~

When Joe made the call to the tribal Elder Henry Ritchie, he felt like there wasn't much of a chance that Henry would be receptive to hearing him out.

"Hi Henry. It's Joe Gonzales over in Fish Lake Valley. I was wondering if I could talk with you about a situation involving a couple of friends of mine. They're a couple of white guys who have a problem and I would like to help them out if I can.

"Joe, it's good to hear from you. I was hoping I would get a chance to talk to you. I want to thank you for the pinion you gave to my old aunt and uncle, Cindy and James over in Furnace Creek. They really appreciated it. They don't have much money and aren't in very good shape to gather wood for themselves, so it was a blessing that you took care of them. Thank you for your generosity. How can I help you?"

~

When the undercover vice officer sat next to her at the race and sports book bar, he thought she might be a working girl from the provocative way she dressed and the lingering eye contact she had with him before he sat down. He ordered a Heineken beer and started to play one of the video poker machines.

"Hi. I saw you walking up to the bar. How's it going?" The thirty-something-year-old prostitute tried not to be too pushy, but desperately wanted to convey her contrived sexual interest in him without looking like she was what she was.

"Hi. I saw you, too, but I didn't want to be too forward. I thought maybe you were with someone. Can I buy you a drink?"

She had to be careful now. If she were too aggressive, it would drive him off. If she wasn't enticing enough, she could lose the john. "Sure, I'll have a white wine."

~

"Joe, you of all people know how we feel about our land. I'm sorry about your friends, but we would *never* let them work the claim. It hurts the land, and if anyone would do it, it would be the Timbisha, not some miners. I'm sorry."

"But Henry, would you at least let them come and present their case to the Tribal Council? You can say no to them then. They're my good friends and they are fine people. At least they'll know that I did everything I could for them. I owe them that much."

"I have to say you are persistent. You don't take no for an answer, do you? Joe, you are a good young man, and I know someday you are going to be a leader. People already respect you. When I was your age, I didn't want to be an Elder, but when I saw injustice and took a stand against it, I found myself at the forefront. You view this as an injustice against your friends, and it is admirable that you are standing up for them. And I appreciate how you are cutting wood for the old people. My old aunt and uncle appreciate it, too. I want you to know that I will try and arrange for them to come and say their piece. But you have to know that even if the other council members allow them to come and speak, the answer will be no. I am only doing this because it was you who asked, and it will fulfill your obligation to your friends. We will never give up our land again and especially to the miners who took it from us before."

"Thank you Henry. I know how everyone feels about our land."

"Trust me, Joe. I'll get a lot of heat from the others just for giving them an audience, about this, but I'll live with it. Just remember, there is no way that we will let them lease the land from us or be a partner with us. It won't happen. I'll leave it up to you to tell them or not to tell them before the meeting. It's up to you. We are only going to do this, because it was you who asked."

"I understand. Thank you." And with that, Joe hung up the phone.

~

She had to be careful now. She put her hand lightly on his thigh and laughed at his joke. "Are you staying here at the casino?"

"Yeah, I'm here for the Consumer Electronics Show. I'm from Grosse Pointe, Michigan. It's my first time in Las Vegas. I'm having a great time. I won $1200 at the blackjack table the first night, and another $326 playing the slots. I've more than covered my expenses so far. What about you? Are you here for the convention, too?"

"No, I'm a local. I just like coming here and hanging out." After two more drinks, and a few more flirtatious laughs, she said," Hey why don't we go on up to your room? It won't cost you as much as your winnings, and I can promise you a lot more fun."

"Whoa! You mean it's going to cost me some money? I've heard about this sort of thing, but I never thought that I would be doing it. How much does it cost?"

When she was being interviewed in the security holding cell in the basement of the casino by the Metro vice sergeant and security sergeant, Scott Alexander, she played her trump card. "If I told you about one of your employees who was ripping you off, do you think I might get a break? I've been splitting the cash with him for letting him know who's got money in safes and who doesn't. Are you interested?"

When they arrested the facilities engineer and searched his locker, they found $4,144, a watch, and a passport belonging to one of the hotel guests. He would be booked on felony theft.

CHAPTER 30: THE MEETING

When Tribal Chairman Henry Ritchie told the other council members about the conversation and Joe Gonzales' request, they reacted as predicted. "I don't mean any disrespect, Henry, but you're asking us to meet with a couple of miners. I don't care if they are good friends of Joe's; I don't see the point. And let's say we do grant them an audience; I think it encourages others to do the same thing. I mean we all have white friends and acquaintances who want to build RV parks, golf courses, and private hunting areas. Remember that developer who wanted to build a big ski lodge up on Lida Summit? Right now they don't even ask to be heard from, because they know how against it we are. I think it opens a door that we don't want opened." Henry had to admit that Vice Chairman Dennis Powers had a point. "Also, I don't even think that you could get a quorum if they all knew in advance what was going to be discussed." Under Article VIII, Section 2, of the Timbisha Constitution no tribal council meeting could take place without at least three of the five council members present.

"Look Dennis, I know that. I'm not talking about having a special meeting; I'm just saying that we allow them to speak at the monthly meeting on Thursday. Joe's a good kid, and I see him as a leader in the not-too-distant future. He's loyal to his friends and he keeps his word. He told his friends that he would, at least, try to get them to be heard. I think that's the kind of man we want to groom for our leadership. Let's face it; we're all getting a little older, and we're not going to be here forever. Look what he took upon himself to do. Nobody asked him to help out the old folks this winter by chopping and delivering wood. That's a lot of work and expense. He did that himself. He even helped out my old aunt and uncle. He did the same for your mother. He's not asking for him. He's asking for his friends. I say we grant his one request. After they say what they have to say, we can say no and that's the end of it. In fact it just might be a good message to get out to others who might be thinking that we could be softening up on the issue of our land use. It says, they listened, and then gave a resounding no. It just reinforces our position."

"Hi Joe, it's Henry. It was a hard sell, but you can tell your friends to come to the meeting this Thursday. Tell them to come around six-thirty. That way we will be done with our monthly business meeting."

"Thank you, Henry. I know it was not something that you wanted to do, but at least old Red and Raymond will know that I followed through."

"Joe, I'm not sure you realize how much the other Council members are against this. I wasn't even sure that I could get a quorum for the meeting when I told them what the agenda was. I think your friends need to know what they are up against, but that's up to you."

"They know what they are up against. I only told them that I would try and get them heard. If the council says no, then they have spoken, and that's it. Thank you again, Henry. I owe you one." The Elder and the unwitting future leader hung up.

When Matt and Alex heard that the Tribal Council had agreed to let Red and Ray speak, they all decided to meet at Pigeon Spring on Thursday morning.

"Joe, I don't know how you pulled this off, but I think you

called in some big favors for this to happen." Matt was astonished.

"I didn't have to call in any favors at all. Henry Ritchie, the Tribal Council Chairman, is just a decent man and wants everyone, even miners, to be treated fairly. But I've got to tell you, Ray, that you shouldn't expect they will agree to anything. The tribe is dead set against going into business with anybody when it comes to our land, so just don't be too disappointed when they say no to whatever proposal you and Red come up with."

"We understand, Joe. At least when we hear it from their own mouths, we'll know that we did everything we could. Me and Red won't have to ask ourselves why we didn't try, or what might have happened if we did get a chance to speak and we didn't." Ray spoke for both of them.

"What ya got there in the jar, Joe? It looks like clay." Red belted out.

"It's called hematite, but the Timbisha call it *tumpisa.* It means, "rock paint." It's red ochre that the Timbisha Tribe is named after. We consider it to be powerful and we believe that it has special healing powers. A long time ago, the Timbisha would paint themselves with it before going into battle. We have an old tradition that if you come to us and ask for something, then the polite thing to do is to offer something when you do the asking. I thought it might be a good gesture when you meet with the council. You guys are going need all luck you have. I figured that it wouldn't hurt anything, and it will look like you're sensitive to the old traditions."

"That's mighty nice of you, Joe. Thanks for the tip." Old Red accepted the jar.

As they started out the door and toward the truck, Alex

called Red back. "I have something for you, too. I never thought that I would allow this to happen, but I want you to take this with you; so much is at stake, it might help. And with that Alex motioned for Red to lean down, and she placed the precious black spearpoint necklace around his neck. "I know that I said it would never leave this place, but I think it should go with you. It might help. Good luck, and we'll see you tonight."

Tensions were high when Henry called the meeting to order. One council member, Steven Wise, even got up and started to leave out of protest when it came time for Red and Raymond to talk. "Steve, I told them that we would listen to them. Come on back and sit down. You can voice your feelings after they've talked."

"I don't even know why we are letting them talk, Henry. It's all a waste of time."

"It might be a waste of time, but we said we would let them say what they came here to say, so come back and sit down."

"Tribal members, we have some guests here tonight who want to address the Tribal Council. I will ask that any comments by members be held until our guests are done speaking. I realize that this is a very controversial subject, but please show them some respect. Thank you. Joe will you please introduce your friends?" Henry sat back down at the table with the rest of the council members.

"Thank you, Chairman Ritchie. Several years ago, I came to meet Red and Raymond. They are prospectors and miners. We all feel the same about the problems we've had in the past with prospectors and miners, but judging them even before meeting them is a lot like saying, 'There's no such thing as a good Indian.' How many times have we all heard that? They're good men and they are honorable people. They are my friends."

With that, both Red and Ray stood up and nodded to the crowd first and then faced the council. Raymond started. "First of all I would like to present Chairman Ritchie and Council members this jar of *tumpisa*. We are very grateful to the council members for allowing us to talk with you today. Henry and two other council members looked at each other and nodded their approval of the thoughtful gesture. The significance of the gift wasn't lost on them. "I know there are many of you who do not agree in permitting us to talk today. I especially want to thank you. I won't take too much of your time.

"Old Red here's been prospecting all of his life out in these parts. I'm sure some of you even know him. He's barely been able to scratch out a living doing what he's been doing. Some time ago, he came across a claim that showed a lot of potential. He cut me in on it so I could help him with it. What we didn't know was that there were some other people who had their eyes on it, and they tried to steal the claim from us. They almost shot us, and until the Sheriff and the FBI helped us, they legally had rights to the claim. They're all in jail now, thanks to the law. There was one last thing that had to be done in order for the claim to be ours, and that was the state survey. When that was done, we found out that the claim was on your property. It's going to produce a lot of gold. In fact it just might be one of the biggest ever in this part of the country. I know that the Timbisha are against mining, because it scars the land. In the past that was true, but the land can be reclaimed nowadays. We are experienced miners and the Timbisha aren't. The Timbisha people could really benefit from all of the wealth of that gold. It's something that could be passed on to your children and their children. You could build schools, hospitals, and provide jobs for a lot of your people. When you decide that you want to take the gold, you are going to need people like me and Red to help you get it. We're local people you can count on and we're not swindlers. What we propose is that we become your partners in the operation. It would be good for the Timbisha, and it would be good for us. Well, that's about all we came here to say, so thank you for your time. Does anyone have any questions for me or Red?"

Steven Wise said, "Yeah. I have a question. Why should we become your partner? We already own it. And we could learn how to mine by ourselves. I don't see any benefit to a partnership for the Timbisha. Right now we have it all; why would we want to split it?

The crowd in the background echoed Steven's sentiment. "Yeah why the hell would we want to do that?" Someone yelled out.

"Yeah! Why do we need anyone else?" Another voice called out.

"Can we please have order?" Henry belted out over the noise and banged his gavel on the wooden block on the desk in front of him. "Now listen. We told them we would hear them out and we did. I say we put it before a vote of the council whether we should become partners with them or not. I make a motion for a vote on it. All in favor of becoming partners with Red and Raymond, please signify so by saying yes and raising your hand." The room was silent. "All against the proposal of entering into a partnership with them, please signify by saying no and raising your hand."

"No!" All five Tribal Council members almost said it in unison, and all five hands shot into the air. The attending crowd cheered. "The no's have it. We will not be partners with the miners. Gentlemen, is there anything else that you wish to say?

If not, this meeting is adjourned."

Red and Raymond walked over to where the council members were seated and bent down to shake each member's hand and individually thank them for their time. As the tall, old man bent over to thank Henry, he saw the ancient relic dangling around his neck. "Red, may I see that?"

"Sure, Henry," and he slipped it off and handed it to him. All five council members examined it one by one, each one showing a surprising reverence for the spearpoint.

"Red, where did you get this? This a very sacred object."

"It's not mine. It belongs to a friend of mine. Her name is Alex. She and her husband own the Pigeon Spring Ranch. I think she found it at the ranch some time back. She told me that it would bring me luck. I guess she was wrong, but I appreciated her doing it anyways."

Henry could feel its power, and he knew all the old stories. As he sat back and took another look at old Red, he was dumbfounded with the overwhelming flood of thoughts that were coming into his head. "Red, can I ask you a couple of questions?"

"Sure Henry, you can ask me anything."

"Where are you from?"

"Well I'm from here. I've lived here all of my life. I was born in a mining shack up near Palmetto. It's long gone, but my mother and father lived there until they died back in the sixties.

"Where were your mother and father from?"

"That's easy. They both were born in Fish Lake Valley. They used to talk a lot about growing up there and what it was like back in the old days. Life was a lot harder for people back then. I remember my grandpa got killed when I was about fifteen. Some drunk outlaw didn't like Irishmen and he shot him for no reason, other than he thought he was an Irishman. The funny thing was though, nobody knew anybody in our family who came from Ireland. I guess maybe there must have been, because a lot of us had this damn red hair."

"You mean you don't know anyone in your background who came from over there?" Henry inquired.

"I'm sure there was, but I'm not aware of anybody. As far as anybody could remember in my family, we've always lived around here."

"Red, I'm sorry for asking so many questions, but I didn't even ask you your last name. Is it Irish or Scottish or something like that?"

"Well, that's the weird thing. It's a Greek name I'm told, but we didn't have any Greeks in the family, either. And that doesn't explain my looks either. My last name is Zadika." When he said the name, Henry dropped the gavel from his hand, and stood and looked up at the old, tall, redhead standing before him. He was bewildered beyond belief.

~

"Matt, why haven't we heard from them? They said that they would come back and let us know how it went as soon as it was over. They should have been back here a couple of hours ago."

"Maybe they had a flat or truck trouble. Or maybe they stopped over at the Boonies Bar in Dyer to commiserate. I'm sure they'll let us know what happened soon. From the way Joe described it, I don't think it's going to be good news anyway. It's just about time for bed. Let's go to sleep. I'm sure we'll hear from them in the morning."

CHAPTER 31: REAWAKENING

The Kennewick man wasn't the only one ever found. In a cave near Reno in 1911 a group of guano miners found mummies, bones, and artifacts buried under four feet of bat excrement. The remains were of a very tall people with red hair. The Paiutes and others had legends about these giant people. According to folklore, they were a troublesome warlike race and the Native American tribes including the Timbisha joined their brother Paiutes in killing them and driving them out. They took their land as their own. They were called "Si-Te-Cah."

~

They spent the entire night in the sweat lodge purifying themselves along with the Timbisha Elders. They both had heard about the ritual, but neither Red nor Raymond thought that he would ever be a part of one. At first the moisture-laden hot air was overpowering, and the sage smoke was stifling. But after a while both found the heat and the sweat brought on by the hot steaming rocks produced a focus in them that neither had experienced before. Most of the prayers and chants were spoken in the Shoshone dialect, but sometimes the prayers were in English. The Elders knew the significance of the event. "Great Spirit, Great Spirit. We have one of our long lost brothers with us. He is as much as a part of this land as we are. Our ancestors have done a great injustice to our brother Si-Te-Cah. We killed them and drove them off their land. Forgive us Great Spirit. It was you and your inspired spearpoint that brought it to light. Thank you for your guidance. We have learned that we can all live in peace. Just as our brother Wovoka knew, purify our bodies and spirits and help us to right the wrongs." All of the Elders took turns in giving thanks and prayers. Even Raymond said a couple of things. He asked Great Spirit to help him overcome Pall Malls and all cigarettes. Old Red felt like a celebrity.

At dawn, they all exited the sweat lodge and looked east at the rising sun. It was a new day.

"We will have a special meeting of the Tribal Council tonight at six o'clock. You can invite your friends Alex and Matt to attend if you want. We'll see you then. Goodbye, my brother Red, and our new friend Raymond." Henry smiled at them as they turned and walked toward Ray's truck.

"Well I have to say, I didn't expect that to happen." Ray offered.

"Yep, sometimes life gets intrestin', don't it?" Red and Raymond headed back to Pigeon Spring.

~

"It looks like you've got war paint on your face, or you're a couple of wide receivers for the Pittsburgh Steelers." Matt observed the red ochre still on their faces from last night's ritual. "What's going on, and where have you guys been?" After they filled Alex and Matt in on the extraordinary events of the previous night, they all ate a breakfast of bacon and eggs and hot coffee. Matt noted that Ray didn't light up after breakfast.

~

"Tribal members and council. We have an unusual situation that has come up. As you all know Red and Raymond from R & R Mining made a proposal to us yesterday to become partners in a joint gold mining operation. Because of our strong position on land use by outsiders, it was soundly rejected. Since then we have discovered some important information that I want to share with all of you." Henry told the story of the destruction and killing of the Si-Te-Cah race by their ancestors, and how old Red was the last of the ancient tribe.

"When we can all learn to live together despite our differences and be at peace with one another, we will be doing Great Spirit's bidding. He doesn't want us to hurt one another or to do bad things to others. We prayed and asked for guidance all last night, and we have made a decision. We have decided *not* to enter into a partnership with R & R Mining."

Matt looked at Red and Raymond, who were equally perplexed by the statement. They thought that they had it all worked out.

"We have decided to try in a very small way to right some of the wrongs that were done in the past. Our ancestors stole the land from our native brothers the Si-Te-Cah, and it is only fitting that when one of the last remaining descendants asks, we do the right thing. We are a just people, and we are all aware of the pain that injustice causes. We have all felt it in our lives. Because of this, we have no choice but to do the right thing. We are giving back what wasn't ours in the first place. We have decided unanimously to deed forty acres of land to Red Zadika. It includes the area of his gold claim." Old Red smiled his nearly toothless smile. He didn't have any problem hearing any of it.

CHAPTER 32: RESOLUTION

"I would like to take the opportunity at this time to dedicate the new Timbisha Medical Center and Clinic to our generous benefactor. Without his support and the generosity of R&R Mining, none of these important projects would have been possible. Because of the good will of this company and its founder, we have been able to tremendously improve our way of life. The trade school, the meetinghouse, and all of the good paying jobs that many of us have are all because of him and his partner. So it is with great pleasure that I hereby dedicate this facility to our brother, the late Ezekiel (Red) Zadika." Tribal Chairman Joseph Gonzales made the announcement before 230 tribal members as they clapped and cheered.

When the elderly Raymond, holding Linda's frail hand, looked out at the cheering crowd, he couldn't have imagined in his wildest dreams the path that his life had taken. It was a remarkable and unpredictable adventure.

After Red was deeded the forty acres, they went right to work and after the first month they hit a lode vein that just didn't give up. The deeper it went, the wider it got until they hit bedrock. Then it started to run up again and to the east. It was a good vein for years. Even after the lode was gone, the claim produced an average of fifteen grams per ton of ore for an output of about 3,750 grams per day. As the years went by, R&R Mining got into other diversified ventures. They had vast real estate holdings, bought into a Las Vegas Casino as a principal, and led the state in the production of solar energy.

Even though they were wealthy, Ray and Linda still lived in a modest house at the north end of Fish Lake Valley. Ray still had his ancient GMC three-quarter-ton pickup, but he had a Cessna 400 Corvalis TT parked on the paved airstrip behind the house, just in case he needed to get somewhere in a hurry. He didn't fly it much anymore himself, but he had a pilot on call if he needed one.

Old Red didn't change his lifestyle much through the years, except he got a high quality hearing aid. He tried a set of dentures once, but couldn't stand having the foreign objects in his mouth. Near the end of his life, he had a little house built for him on the property where he had the old camper trailer parked near the road toward Sylvania. He remained the humble man that he always was. He died a peaceful death in his sleep early one bright spring morning. His old heart just quit beating.

Even well into his mid eighties, Matt stayed active at the ranch in spite of his arthritic right knee. A regular shot of cortisone usually freed him up until the next flare up. Brio, the criminal gelding and the mare T had died years earlier, so Matt bought a smooth-riding Tennessee walker as a replacement. The smoother gait didn't rattle his old bones as much. After he retired from the casino business, he took about a year off and spent most of his time with Alex and the occasional great-grandchild at Pigeon Spring. Even though there was always work to do at the ranch, and he enjoyed it, he craved being with working people, so he ran for Esmeralda County Justice of the Peace. He was elected by a landslide, mostly because nobody else ran against him. He liked the sound of Judge.

"You might be a judge, but you still need to take out the garbage." Alex never let him get too big for his britches.

He missed his old partner Charlie. He had passed away

three years ago, doing what he loved. After eighteen holes of golf, and while sitting at the nineteenth, he went suddenly while drinking one of his famed margaritas. Matt always thought they would kill him, and they did just that.

~

Alex always knew that there would be an end to it someday, but when her grandson Thomas, now a successful computer engineer with a family of his own showed up at the cabin door, she could see the redness in his swollen eyes. "Nana, he's gone." He told her about the traffic accident that took Matt's life out on U.S. 95 just outside of Goldfield. Fortunately, no one else was injured. He ran off the road and onto the soft shoulder. He over-corrected, and the SUV rolled. Even though he had his seatbelt on, he didn't survive the trauma. He was gone even before the ambulance got there from Tonopah.

CHAPTER 33: SAYING GOODBYE

It had been eight years since she had gotten the devastating news about Matt, but Alex had managed to go on just like all of the others who found themselves without their life partner after so many years. She missed him deeply and was grateful for the long and wonderful adventure they had shared for so many years, but now it was time.

"Thomas, can you drive me up to Pigeon Spring this weekend? I'd like to spend the night if you think you can spare the time. It's been a long time since I've been there, and I just might not be able to do it if I wait any longer."

"Of course, Nana. Colleen and the kids were planning on going to the beach this weekend anyway. I'll pick you up Saturday morning."

When Thomas pulled up in the antique F-350 Ford diesel, Alex smiled as she remembered the first time saw him sitting up on Matt's lap behind the steering wheel of the big truck. After Matt died, Thomas took the vehicle and maintained it all of these years. It still looked good.

When they arrived at the cabin, she looked over at the towering cottonwood trees and was pleased to see two red-tailed hawks preparing their nest. They always returned.

The cabin looked well maintained, too. She wanted the grandchildren to use it, and their presence throughout the years had kept the vandals away. Thomas helped his elderly grandmother up the stairs and into the cabin. He knew what she was focused on. There it was, sitting in the glass case above the fireplace just like she left it some time ago.

After dinner, they sat by the fireplace and talked about Matt, Charlie, old Red, Raymond, and Linda. They laughed a lot and they both cried a little. "Thomas will you please get that old spearpoint down for me? I think I want to hold it again."

That night the ancient relic talked to Alex again for the last time.

She saw a young Matt grinning at her with his youthful smile. He took her by the hand, and they walked past the old corrals and watched Brio doing his torturous teasing routine with the mares. They walked up past the spring and watched the hawks tending to their nest. They climbed the ridge and looked out toward the stark snowcapped Sierra Nevada silhouetted against the brilliant blue sky. And they walked down the ridge behind the cabin hand-in-hand to the spot where she found the spearpoint so many years ago.

The next morning, she knew what she had to do. "Thomas, I don't know if I can manage this, but I want you to help me to get to the top of the ridge. A long time ago, your grandfather and I made a trail that we could use when we got really old to get up there. I guess it's that time. I'm really old, and I'll need your help. We'll go slowly.

It took some time to get there, but somehow they managed. When they got to the spot Alex said, "Thomas, will you please leave me here alone for a little while? I'll be all right."

"Sure, Nana. I'll be back in a little while." After she was certain that he was gone, she took the relic off of the necklace and after clinging to it for a few more moments, reverently placed it where she took possession of it many years before. She placed it next to an old twisted pinion pine just like she had found it.

Alex looked south toward the cottonwood stand, and then west toward the snow-covered peaks of the Sierra Nevada still standing guard like they always would. "Goodbye."

EPILOGUE

When Kelly first got the call that she had inherited a large parcel of property in Nevada, she had to admit she was intrigued. She recalled the stories from her grandfather about his days on the ranch as a child. He said that his grandfather, Thomas, spent his young years there, too, when it was being developed over a century ago. She tried to picture what it must have been like. None of the modern conveniences existed back then. It must have been a difficult way to live. They had to drive cars and trucks with gasoline motors and travel for hours to get there. How did they do it? And what would she do with it? She and her husband were firmly entrenched in the lifestyle of a modern professional couple living in coastal California. At least she should go there for a couple of days and see it before she sold it.

"How old do you think this shack is?"

"Before he died, I think I remember my grandfather saying that it was built about 150 years ago by somebody in the family. He said that he started coming here with his grandfather when he was a little kid. Anyway, it's been in the family for generations. I guess a long time ago it was an Indian camp, and they had a gold plant or something down there by that big pile of rocks and wood. There's a lot of history to it I guess." As they walked the ridgeline and took in the westward vista, Kelly noted, "It is a beautiful view of the mountains from here, isn't it?" She stopped abruptly. "Speaking of Indians, look at this. It looks like some sort of arrowhead. That's funny. How could I have missed it?" She had walked the same path several times over the last couple of days, and didn't notice it. Maybe somebody lost it. Kelly studied it for a few moments from a distance. She didn't know why, but she hesitated before picking it up. Then she reached for it and touched it.

The *connection* had been made. Now she was a part of it. The sculptor, the warriors who used it, the flesh of the animals it had pierced. Those who had possessed it: All of them. Now she was *connected.*

That night the mute relic talked for the first time in a long time.

"You have noticed that everything an Indian does is in a circle, and that is because the power of the world always works in circles, and everything tries to be round … The sky is round, and I have heard that the earth is round like a ball, and so are all the stars. The wind, in its greatest power, whirls. Birds make their nest in circles, for theirs is the same religion as ours … Even the seasons form a great circle in their changing, and always come back again to where they were. The life of man is a circle from childhood to childhood, and so it is in everything where power moves."

Black Elk, Oglala   Sioux Holy Man

THE END

About the Author

Herman Groman is a retired FBI Special Agent and is the current director of security at large Las Vegas casino/hotel. While in the FBI, he specialized in working deep long-term undercover operations as an undercover agent in the areas of organized crime and narcotics. He also served as the agent in charge of several high-profile public official corruption investigations. Later on in his FBI career, he was a team leader of one of the FBI Special Operations Groups. The specialized group conducted surveillances of major terrorist cell groups and their associates. He served in the infantry in Vietnam and was awarded the purple-heart and bronze star for valor. He resides in Las Vegas with his wife. They have two adult daughters and four grandchildren.

Lightning Source UK Ltd.
Milton Keynes UK
01 June 2010

154973UK00001B/41/P